CONOCIMIENTOS
PRESS

Street of Too Many Stories

Denise Chávez

CONOCIMIENTOS
PRESS

Book design by ash good.
Cover inspired by a photograph taken by Daniel Zolinsky.

Published by Conocimientos Press, LLC
San Antonio, Texas

ISBN: 978-1-961794-00-9

CONOCIMIENTOSPRESSLLC.COM

RESIDENTS ON ENCANTADA STREET

The Fuentes Family

Reymundo "Mundo" Fuentes, *father*
Ermelinda "Erme" Fuentes, *mother*
Victoria "Vicky," Fuentes, *daughter*

The Chapa Family

Rafael "Rafa" Chapa, *father*
Mariaelena "Mari" Contreras, *mother*
Linda Chapa, *daughter*

The Stillman Family

Robert "Bob" Stillman, *father*
Leticia "Lety" Casados Stillman, *mother*
Michael Stillman, *son*
Clemson "Clem" Stillman, *son*

The Blanco Family

Joe Blanco, *father*
Senaida "Sen" Blanco, *mother*

Ayudantes/Helpers

Adelaida Huerta
Lázara Domínguez
Emma Regalado
Analuisa Peralta
Chole Contreras
Betty Lu "Grammy" Ruckman
Pasajero, *a dog*
Sammy, *a cat*

Symbol for Rain

INTRODUCTION

A small town. A small street. Four Families. Encantada, New Mexico.

Reymundo "Mundo" Fuentes once lived on Encantada Street, but Mundo's alcoholism and womanizing took its toll. He and his wife, Ermelinda "Erme," divorced when their daughter, Victoria, "Vicky" was a child. Vicky became her father's custodian and neighbor when Mundo became ill and moved back, assuming her mother's role of caretaking.

Neighbors Rafael "Rafa" Chapa and his wife Marialena "Mari" have nothing in common. She comes from a small village in México, speaks no English, does not know how to drive, has never bought her own clothes, or shopped for food. Mari spends her days behind the curtains of her house, cleaning and watching American soaps. Rafa began abusing their daughter, Linda, as a young child. As an adult Linda finally left home, only to return time and time again, to the place of her haunting, looking for an ephemeral peace with her past. In the novel's interconnected stories, Linda seeks healing through every form of therapy, finally confronting and resolving her legacy of family abuse.

The Stillman family lives down the street from the Fuentes and Chapa's. Bobby and his wife Lety have too many children. Lety's mother. Adoración, thirty years confined to a wheelchair, lives in the laundry room of the house, amongst her memories, waiting for her favorite son, "Robe" to return home. Clem Stillman, the oldest brother, outwardly charming, sets an abusive example for his younger brother, Michael, seducing many of his mother's helpers, women of all ages from México. Michael becomes an alcoholic, a member of the Arid Club, an AA group that he attends with his neighborhood childhood friend, Linda

Chapa, who moves in and out of his life, the two of them clinging to each other for stability.

Another Encantada Street neighbor, Joe Blanco lives on one side of the house he shares with his wife, Senaida "Sen." Married for too many years, Joe often reads the newspaper in his car, spied upon by his elderly neighbor, Mundo Fuentes, whose vantage point is the large picture window that he looks out daily to see the small world of Encantada Street. Joe and Sen seldom cross each other's path.

An older woman Adelaida Huerta, a Mexican woman from Juárez, works as a housekeeper, nanny, cook, and caregiver to the neighborhood families, moving from one house to another, attending to each families changing needs.

The Street is a character and speaks to the reader, telling us about its long history, the creatures that lived in the sea, and then on the earth and then moved on. The spirits of Encantada Street return from time to time, to peer inside the houses of the families that once lived on that street. They dance and sing, curious to see what is going on with the living.

The symbol for rain highlights each section of these interconnected stories. Rain and its emotional, spiritual, and physical equivalents are what everyone longs for—respite, blessing, understanding, mercy, and forgiveness. Where is Encantada Street? On the U.S./Mexican border, that liminal space of challenge and hope.

The novel is an homage and prayer to those who have endured the legacy of family dysfunction and found their way toward understanding the deep and solid parts of their intact core selves.

There are many people to thank for this book. I am a blessed child. Their names are written on the western wind and in the gentle rain that washes their footsteps clean.

—*Denise Chávez*

Pa' La Vecina . . .

Most of the time he wanted to think about women. The women he'd known. Yes, in the Biblical way. There were many of them. He wished he'd made a list. Once, he tried to talk to his daughter, Victoria, about all the women he'd made love to. She didn't want to hear about it. Well, he couldn't blame her. Probably talking about other women besides her mother wouldn't interest her. Not that he talked about Ermelinda much to her or to anyone. They'd been divorced for many years. He would have a hard time explaining to his daughter what happened. What had happened? Oh, he only knew too well. Let's move on.

He twisted from one side to another. The rented hospital bed was still hard after all this time.

He didn't want to think about his past now or at least for too long.

Suddenly, for no reason, he thought of Pasajero, the dog he had before his family moved to California. They didn't stay there long, but by the time the family came back Pasajero was long gone.

Mundo had been inconsolable when his father told him the dog had to stay behind.

But Pasajero's familia! He's familia!

Ni familia ni que familia. He's just a dog. An animal. They don't know or care. Someone comes up and gives him food, they'll take off with them, and you'll never see them again.

He's my dog, my dog! I love him!

No, mi'ijto. Así es.

Mundo cried in the room he shared with his two brothers, the girls down the hallway. His parents' room at the back of the house.

He's just a dog. Animals don't have souls.

But he's my dog. My dog. My dog. He's familia!

What had happened to Pasajero? Did his father leave him with someone? Or did he just drop him off by the side of the road a distance away to disorient him? Did he take him to the river like the bad priest who killed cats? Did they leave him with parientes, family members who loved animals and had children? Where did Pasajero go? Was he happy in his new home? Did he miss Mundo? Mundo loved him, and Pasajero loved him as well.

Pasajero. The word means traveler. Turns out Mundo was the one who went away. He didn't want to go so far away, but his father Nicanor said that it was a good opportunity and that he would find steady work. Here there was no work, and if there was work, it was in los files, picking cotton, or on a farm. How could a man with a family of seven make money working that kind of back-breaking work for so little money? No, it wasn't possible to stay in that small dusty town named Encantada and serve others. Enchanted? The town was never enchanted! Nicanor's cousin, Raúl, had been to San Diego and said it was a beautiful place. The ocean was nearby and there were fruit trees everywhere. It's a paradise, primo. So, what's holding you back?

Paquita, Nicanor's wife, was pregnant again, and he was afraid to leave with her so near the birth, but they had to, there was nothing left for them in Encantada. California! The land of opportunity and hope. Everyone headed in that direction, and no one was looking back to the poverty of their lives in New Mexico. What did they have there that they couldn't have in California? The move would be good for him and for the children. He would find work right away, that's what Raúl said, and the children, ay, they would forget they were ever poor. California! And besides, they had family there. Their cousins would help them until they got a place of their own and he would pay them back, yes, he would. He'd heard from his prima, Dolores, and she was expecting them.

The children were excited. He didn't think Paquita cared much for the move. The pregnancy wasn't her easiest. She was tired all the time and irritable. And she was a cold and harsh woman to begin with, so things were bad. It wasn't a good idea to leave with the winter coming on. But then again, California was warmer. Things would stabilize once they got there. Everything would settle down. Paquita would be busy with the baby, the other children. And he would find a good job. They would be happy there. They would be far away from the dust, the poverty, and the hard life that gave him so little. He would sell off the remaining land he had there. It was good land, but he didn't want to work it. Let his primos be the farmers. He was an adventurer. Not a farmer. Nicanor had no desire to be a servant to farm animals and the plow. If only things had worked out with the gold mine. He had such hopes. He had found the traces, but that was all . . . traces.

Finally, the day came when Mundo had to say goodbye to Pasajero. He thought he would never stop crying.

Boys don't cry, they don't Mundo, his father said to him. His older brother, Felipe, made fun of him and that only made things worse. He clung to Pasajero. He told him he was so sorry. So sorry. And then he cried some more. It's so hard to say goodbye. Really a forever goodbye is the hardest thing in the world. All his life Mundo had been saying goodbye. His was a goodbye life. He was only twelve but already he'd had the goodbyes of a person much older. He knew what it was to cry in his room late at night and wonder how ugly the world was and how evil people could be. He promised himself that when he got older, he wouldn't cry for anyone: man, woman, or animal. He never wanted to cry again like he had when he was twelve. That was the year his family moved to California and left everything he loved behind. It was a hard year and a hard time. He always hated the month of December. It was a cold month, and he didn't like to be cold. Christmas didn't mean anything to him especially since it was in December, the coldest, hardest time of all times.

The worst things happened in December. He didn't want to think about that horrible December when he was apprenticed to that man in California. He wouldn't think about it now. He couldn't think about it now.

Paquita hadn't wanted her husband, Nicanor, to send Mundo to work for her husband's compadre as an apprentice. El Compadre was a shoemaker, and he had a good business. He also did repair work on saddles and farm equipment. He had a steady income, and this is what prompted Nicanor to decide to send Mundo to El Compadre to learn a trade. It was too far away, Paquita begged. Your son is weak, he needs special care. And that's why he must go away, Nicanor said firmly, he's soft like a woman, and needs to grow up. Look how he behaved with that dog. What was his name?

With tears, Paquita and her son parted ways. Mundo was gone that winter. When he came back, he was not the same son who had left. Mundo was distant and cold whereas he had once been a warm and loving child. He had become cynical and rude. It was hard for Paquita to see. All the family suffered because of him.

What had happened to him? To Nicanor there seemed to be nothing wrong, but to Paquita her son Mundo's life had been turned upside out, inside out and turned dark. Sometimes she could hear him crying out in terror in his sleep. No, no, no, please, no, he would whimper. What had happened to her son? He would never be the same loving child he once had been. He became cruel to animals where once he had loved them. He had once treated everyone with respect and courtesy and now he was rude, even to her, and this broke her heart. He grew up too fast, started smoking and then drinking and became a haughty and careless young man. He was handsome, like all her boys, and he treated women badly. He was to break many hearts and not care, and he almost died in a car accident and each life lesson became a milestone of bitterness for him.

What had happened at El Compadre's house? Mundo never spoke of it. People didn't talk to each other the way they do now. Mothers never talked to their sons because a mother's role was to step aside and serve her husband and then her children. It was rare to hear a parent tell a child that they were loved. She could never tell Mundo how much she loved him. Her husband, Nicanor, and all the world of men forbade it.

What had happened to Mundo?

She suspected.

But she would never know. It would break her heart to know. A mother should know. A mother would know. Wouldn't she? But if it was true, what would she say?

Pasajero. The Traveler. The dog who stayed at home. The dog who was left behind. The dog the family forgot about. The dog he was still thinking about so many years later as he lay in his rented hospital bed.

The bed was at the back of the house, in the corner room. It was a good room if you wanted to live in your daughter's house with all kinds of old leftover women who took care of you twenty-four hours a day. Women who got you up each morning, changed your diapers, walked you to the bathroom, then checked on you all the time. It's hard to take a good goddamn shit at a prescribed time and on command. No sir, it was a bad life. Una vida arrastrada. A dragged-out ugly life.

Mundo's father, Nicanor, was a dreamer. Many felt he never amounted to much. He'd lost all the land he once had and to his own disgust and shame, all his cousins became wealthy farmers.

The family moved to California in early December. It was a cold, long trip. His mother, Paquita, gave birth to a tiny sick baby who grew up to be a tiny sick little girl. They stayed in California for a while, however long it was for Paquita to give birth, watch her grow, and then bury the little girl. When Mundo got back to Encantada, it was a different world. Everyone had been touched, both by magic and by fire. The family would never be the same. The little girl's name was Elisabet. They called her Betita. She was a sweet child, and everyone loved her more than they loved each other. She was the culmination of that hope that they all carried those long miles from Encantada to the state line, and then further; she was the hope of a new life. To have her leave the way she did, coughing and crying softly, and in great distress, was a sorrowful thing. She withered away from the influenza and spewed blood out of her mouth and nose. It was a terrible thing to see. Someone young or old never recovers from the ugly, agonizing death of a beloved child. A child everyone adored. When Elisabet died, that's when Nicanor decided to return home.

And what does this all have to do with you now, Mundo? What does it matter your sister died so many years ago and when you came back home your dog was gone?

Celia! Mundo yelled out. Celia! Was that her name? Or was it María? Whatever the hell her name was, she was slow. He needed to go to the bathroom and now! Get me up, get me up! Dammit, get me up. Where's my daughter? Where is Victoria? Where is she?

Mr. Fuentes, calm down, Celia or María or Cata or Juana called out to him. Calm down. Your daughter's working. She'll be back later. Now just rest, rest. It's time for your nap. You don't need to go to the bathroom. You just went. And besides, you have a diaper on.

I need to go to the bathroom, cabrona! Take me to the goddamn bathroom. What time is it? Cata! Dammit, Cata, I have to go to the bathroom I don't care what you say!

It's time for your nap. You always take a nap at this time of the day, Mr. Fuentes. Vicky will be back later. She's working. You don't want to bother her, do you? She's a good daughter.

Rafa had wanted his woman to be beautiful. And she was. Marielena was a beauty even in a small town full of beautiful women. That's how it was in Poponango, that remote village in México. Rafa met her there when he went to visit his mother's cousins that summer. Marielena was a neighbor girl. She was sixteen and already dazzling, with a luxurious and full body and long dark hair. And she was sweet and even better, quiet. She knew how to step back and let others take the lead. He needed someone who knew her place and wouldn't make a fuss. He didn't like drama, unnecessary words, stupid action, and useless rambling on. Life was simple or it should be. He'd had enough wild drama in his parent's home and never wanted to repeat the ridiculous spectacle.

Rafael "Rafa" Chapa was a small man, not at all handsome, with large ears and a little belly. He had a slight curvature of the spine which made him look like a little toad, hunched out of necessity. He looked older than his years. He was twenty-four when he met Marielena Contreras and wooed her away from whatever other suitors were hanging around her with the promise of moving to El Norte. There were a few other admirers, mostly at a distance, because her father kept a close watch. But once he'd spoken to her father, Don Eliseo, it was a done deal. She would become his wife. He did have a few good traits then, he thought, but he just couldn't remember them now. It was a long time ago when he brought his bride to Los Estates and settled her in the small house they were to live in while she raised their children, three girls and a boy. One of the girls was beautiful like her mother, one of them was plain and overweight, and the other dressed like a man, acted like a man, and left home when she was in high school, never to return. The son, well, he was the only ray of hope for Rafa. But that was another story. It had still been worth it. Marielena was a good wife: quiet, unassuming, strong but delicate, a hard worker, a good cook, someone who didn't complain. She never got in his way and kept out of his things and his life. She was undocumented, never got her papers, he never felt it was necessary. She was almost invisible to the world, and it was good. She never really learned English, and it was probably good, although maybe she did speak a little, he wasn't sure. She had a few words he imagined, but if she did speak English, she never spoke those words to him. She liked to watch television during the day, and he would find her following along as if she understood everything that was being said. So—who knows, maybe she did speak English.

American soaps were nothing like their Mexican counterparts. Americans were very dull Marielena thought. When they raise their voices, you can't understand why they are so excited and when they cry you can't believe their tears. When a Mexicano cries, they cry from the inside out as if their guts were being pulled out and wrenched from them and left there to dry, a heaving mass of blood and guts. There are no llantos like that of the Mexicanos. Just attend a velorio in my hometown, that's what I'm talking about. Tears, repentant and true, hot, slippery, slimy, and without shame, not the false tears of timid and overwrought actors who don't know the sorrows of the world. Americanos don't know how to cry, I say. And yet, they have so much to cry about. You'd think, yes, you'd think they would know how to behave when grief looks them in the face and says hello. Pero no. No. For this and for other reasons I am glad I stayed a Mexicana. And even though I've lived here all these years, I haven't lived here, if you know what I mean, Chapa. I am not a part of this insane world called Los Estates.

They called each other by their last names, it never varied.

So, what are you, Contreras, a philosopher? What are you talking about, you didn't even finish high school? What do they call it? La prepa in México. What do you know about anything?

I've learned a little living with you, Chapa. Notice I say a little.

Oh sí, what then? What have you learned?

I've learned that men here or there or anywhere never change. They never want to change. With you, women are always in the background. A step behind the man. If there is a man around, the woman assumes the lesser position, always, in a shadow place to his left—of course, the shadow side where the Darkness lives. Timid and flat-chested, all the little white brides stand behind their men, who shield their stern faces from the sun. Look at all the photographs of the Gringo men and Gringo women and then look at the Mexicanos. To a Mexicana/o what is the most derogatory thing you can call an American? Gringo? Gabacho? It's the same. The women are behind, always behind. Their faces are washed out, sad, without emotion. What life awaits them in a place like this or any other? I never expected much from you, Chapa. And I never got much except for my children. And I suppose that's enough. Yes, it is. Or it has to be. I've accepted that. I've known all along that my children, notice I call them *my* children, are the closest thing to God for me. Maybe they are my God. They are a God I believe in, anyway. And you, I have no idea who your God is. *If* there is a God in your life. *If* there ever was a God, who would that be? I don't know.

Marielena had this conversation with Chapa every day except it was all in her mind. She wanted to say all those things to him, but she couldn't. She'd stopped speaking once she crossed the border in Juárez and her voice never came back. She would live in Chapa's house for over fifty years, but she hardly spoke. She didn't speak English, she didn't drive, she didn't do the grocery shopping, and she didn't buy her clothing, or her children's. Chapa did everything for her and for him and for them. And she, Marielena Contreras, stayed at home, cleaning house and then when she was done, which was usually early because all she did was clean, she would turn on the television without sound and watch the white people on the screen try and talk to each other. When they cried, and it seemed to be often, they weren't real tears, it was only the make-believe suffering of people who didn't know what true suffering is or would ever be. She wanted to feel sorry for all those blonds on television and the men with blue eyes who had tried to love them but didn't. Many of them had thin hair or wore hair pieces or were sure to have false teeth that never seemed to fit their mouths. She couldn't see that the women saw in those weak and impotent men. What does a woman see in a man after all? What attracts a woman? Hair, teeth, good skin, a robust body, charm, a melodious voice, whispers in the night, a touch like velvet on her skin, salty kisses hot and deep, the never-ending promise of company, perhaps a sense that no matter what, there would be peace and tranquility and rest? Every woman wants to eventually find a man who will leave her in peace. That's what she wanted then, and that's what she still wanted. To be left alone.

Ay, Chapa! Chapa was her guardian, her gatekeeper. It was he who trained and groomed her and then let her sit in her hot bed of a house in the middle of the afternoon without worrying about the world except what the stupid Gringo people on the television hissed and then yelled at each other, mouthing curses that formed like bubbles in the air and moved away, down the street, the street with too many stories. She knew her little street from the inside out and was sometimes grateful for the rest inside her clean little fortress. She knew the world out there was too much, too hard, too ugly, too evil, and that she couldn't take it for very long. And yet, sometimes she hated her life so much that she wanted to run away like María Elva, her middle daughter, never to return to them. Lucky girl, she got away. Run, mi'ija, run! You have everything you need to speak the truth and to live the truth even though it isn't the truth for most women. I will never understand how you turned from men to women and became a man in front of me. But I'm glad, mi'ija. This way you won't have to stand in the shadows, to the left of all men, in the dark shadowy place where the demons reside and where Death lives, watching us. Good for you. And yes, I'm proud. That's what I'd say if you returned. María Elva, I'm proud of you for becoming the man I never could become. And for becoming a woman that doesn't cry in silence. I believe that what is unsaid eventually screams inside of us, mi'ija. Listen to me. Can you hear me? I don't want to have you scream in silence the way I have for so many years. If I could turn up the sound on the television, I would. But I can't. I don't like the harshness of the sounds, the words that pierce and tear people and the world apart. In silence I can imagine the words and change them. That's how I do it. That's how I've done it to survive. If I could listen, I would. But I can't. It's better this way. Believe me, mi'ija. You don't want to scream that way—your mouth not even moving.

Their house always smelled of urine. The children wet their beds into their teens. It couldn't be helped—the air was saturated, fecund, overripe. It was a sad house despite the constant noise and movement of too many children, and oftentimes other relatives who came to visit and stayed a week or a month or sometimes years. Thank God they didn't have pets. There was no room for pets. The girls slept together in several rooms, the boys on the other side of the house. The wife's brother was only there occasionally, and he slept here and there, in the room with the television, or on the living room couch. The grandmother, Adoración or Mamá Adora as she was called by her family, had her own room. It was full of her things, chucherías—all sorts of old lady knickknacks—ancient and yellowed birthday cards, desiccated Palm Sunday palms, rosaries of all sizes, a box full of soft dusty white handkerchiefs and shelves full of photographs of people no one but the grandmother remembered. It was a room crowded with memory, loss, and longing. It was also crowded with plastic laundry baskets. Adora's room if you wanted to call it that, was the laundry room. She shared the room with a washer and dryer in one corner near a door that led to the kitchen. The old woman's job was to fold the laundry. The washing machine was going all the time with so many people in the house. She was very busy.

The washing machine was old and made a rattling noise like it was being dragged across the floor. It was the sound of metal scraping a cement floor, jarring, and clanging. It chugged and panted and worked all day long as the house's inhabitants constantly did laundry. The washing machine never stopped except late at night when people went to bed. The old woman too, contributed much to the wash loads. She wore diapers and had been incontinent for over thirty years.

An industrial iron was nearby, in the kitchen. It was large and scary to those who saw it for the first time. It was something you would see at a professional dry cleaner. How anyone managed to use it seemed incomprehensible. Who exactly used it? The mother, whose name was Leticia or "Lety" to her family, was always busy running after someone. But she was not the ironing type. The industrial iron had been a good idea, but it mostly sat unused. Ironing took time and concentration, something Lety had little of.

Lety never wore dresses or pants in the house. And most assuredly, if she did, they were permanent press or polyester. Most of the time she wore a nightgown and over that a bata, or housedress that was popular in that era. Something like an apron and yet more like a dress, the standard bata covered up and allowed the wearer to go braless, without underwear, if that is what they so wished. In other words, it covered up most of the body and allowed the wearer to be free of anything confining. Lety Stillman, or Momma as everyone called her, didn't need to worry about fashion day or night because the bata covered it all. She had several of them that she rotated. When one was being washed and then folded by Adora, another one was being pulled out of her closet to take its place.

So, then imagine a house that smelled like a nursery full of babies, or a room filled with old men and women in a badly kept nursing home, or perhaps, a house that was heavy with the smell of too many unwashed bodies, all in different stages of growth and decomposition. Imagine the one small dark bathroom that had its own smell of too many people using it, with a drippy toilet that exuded a ripe and pungent urine smell, a shower you were afraid to peer into, and then forced to step into from time to time, and a wash basin that was used by so many people that it was hard to find which toothbrush was yours and to hang on to it. This was the Stillman house.

The house had two refrigerators and two freezers. The main refrigerator was in the kitchen, and one was in the pantry next to a large freezer, and there was another freezer at the back of the house, in a storage shed. Every one of them was in use. The freezer in the pantry was full of ice cream because the family sat down every night to eat ice cream together, it was their nightly ritual. If you were lucky and happened to be at the house when it was time to eat ice cream, you were blessed.

The kitchen had a large wall shelf that held many cereal boxes of all kinds. Some were full, some of them were nearly empty, and some were unopened. The children knew that cereal was always available. With so many people coming and going throughout the day, each with their separate and distinct schedules, it was good to have cereal and other types of food that were accessible, readily obtainable, and fast, and that anyone of any age could graze on when necessary. What do you feed seven children and any number of adults? Whatever and whenever you can.

The Stillman children were half Anglo and half Other. Some of them identified with their Mexican American grandparents, many of the children did not. Some of them identified with the Oklahoma Stillman clan, all of them lanky big-boned soft-spoken people like Bob Stillman. Some of them spoke Spanish, most of them did not. Some of them had accents like the Stillman clan, a hesitant and lingering southern drawl and others spoke quickly and with dramatic staccato inflection like Lety and her people. The children that grew up with the grandparents were more likely to speak Spanish than the younger children. The ones that did speak Spanish didn't speak it fluently, but in the world, they grew up in, it didn't matter. They were the Stillmans.

Robert "Bob" Stillman came into his wife Lety's family as an outsider. Lety was short, petite, with curly hair and a light skin color. She didn't look like a Mexican, whatever a Mexican looked like in Encantada in those years. Bob's family would have said they looked like brown wetback beaners before they met Lety, the love of their son Robert's life. Lety spoke good English but wasn't much of a cultured person. She had dropped out of school as a sophomore in high school to work. Thankfully in those years she had mastered typing and shorthand. Bob had attended a few semesters of college, but he, too, went to work early. Bob was tall and handsome with a muscular body, and he was to everyone in Encantada, Anglo. An Anglo in those days was a White man before they were called Whites. Both of their families opposed the marriage. Bob was a Protestant; Lety was a Catholic. He was younger, she was older. And yet, they were an ideal couple. Lety was always in charge, and he was there to help her. She was a stay-at-home mother and he sold cars and then later, was a realtor. When he changed religions for her it was easy, not a hardship. He became a very good Catholic the more he aged, as she lapsed and rarely went to Mass. She was too busy for mass, and yes, she knew God forgave her she thought as she loaded another round of soggy laundry. Someone had wet the bed again!

Michael Stillman had to get out of the house. It was stifling. It was getting dark earlier as the weather began to change from fall to winter. He needed to get some fresh air. Almost every day he went on a walk around the neighborhood. Nothing much to see most of the time. But it was better than being cooped up with everyone. He wondered when he would finally get out of the house and be on his own. He was seventeen and he didn't want to be tied to his parents much longer. His father was a pathetic drone who lumbered through life selling real estate and his mother had nothing to do but nurse and procreate, procreate, and nurse. He didn't particularly like his brothers and sisters. And if you came down to it, and he did have occasion to really ponder the vast conundrum of life with his large family, he really didn't like most of them. They were bothersome and worse yet, needy.

Michael left the house through the back door. Momma wouldn't see him leave and probably wouldn't miss him. She might even be relieved that one less person was around to make noise and attempt to be heard. She had the little kids to attend to, as well as Adora, and her brother Roberto, who everyone called Robe, who was visiting until his divorce became final. Robe was funny, but sad, and would sit out on the back porch and drink beer most nights. He never spoke much but would quietly get drunk and then fall into a hard sleep on the couch in the television room. It was bothersome to have him around because Momma wouldn't let the kids turn on the television if her brother was in there snoring loudly. He wouldn't have noticed the noise, truly, but there you had it. When Robe was around, all stopped to relegate their wishes for him. And then suddenly, without warning, he would leave and his mother, Adora, would be screeching out to her favorite son and zas! He'd be gone until next time, next break up, or next threatened divorce proceedings. He was a human yo-yo of suffering.

And yet, Michael or "Mikey" as everyone called him, wanted to make sure he was back in time for ice cream. He left when it was still light out. Stepping out the back door the smell of red chile assailed him. He deeply inhaled the pungent and sweet smell of the chile pods being roasted and processed at the nearby food plant. Mingling with that rich dark smell of seed and pod was the underlying odor of cumin. He loved to smell the night. Rich. Full. Mysterious. All seemed right and good. He told himself: just smell the air and forget for a while the yawning overwhelming fact: he just didn't belong to these people. He was different. Sometimes he loved them, but most of the time he hated them. He just didn't like how dependent they were on each other. They were people who leaned on each other too much. He wanted a delineation, a definition, he wanted to be himself, not one of them, a Stillman. And who were the Stillman, anyway, but people caught between cultures, languages, and identities. Who was Michael Stillman, anyway? What made him different from his parents and siblings in that crowded human nest that he inhabited?

The night was warm for November. It was the full moon that gave off a certain tender glow. The street was illuminated and somehow, he felt it was inviting him to walk its length. It was a familiar neighborhood. The cats crossed the road in the same places. The dogs barked at the same houses. He would call out to them softly. Shh, shh, it's all right. Settle down now. And the dogs would stop barking and the cats would saunter up to him for they knew he loved them, each and every one. He didn't have any pets of his own, but he did love animals. He couldn't imagine having a pet at home. No money to feed them, or to take them to the vets. Not only that, but his parents would never allow it. They were too busy with humans to imagine an animal living with them as a companion. No more companions were needed. What they needed was a clearing out, a breath and respite for the ones who did live in the house.

The night air felt good. Michael had to get away often. The walk was a daily thing, and it was needed. He would check up on the latest developments in the neighborhood. See who was home and what was left undone or started. The across-the-street neighbor still had two lawn mowers outside his house near the front door. They had been out there for months and still no one thought of taking them inside into a shed. It was getting cold and nearing the end of grass cutting season, and still the twin lawnmowers rested near the Samaniego's front door. The Álvarez, on the other hand, still had last year's Christmas tree in the front yard. It was totally desiccated, a yellow-brown color, and was rammed up against the house behind a camper that was parked in the front yard. Michael meant to move it into some nearby garbage bin as he was tired of seeing it just lying out there in the front yard, but he never did. Now you couldn't get to it anymore because of the camper shell that blocked it. The Olivas' mop was also in its regular spot next to the entrance of their house waiting for someone to take it inside and clean. The Smith's front yard still looked like a haunted house with all sorts of scary things in the large front picture window, remnants of too many Halloweens gone by. There was a ceramic skull with glowing eyes, as well as a golden Buddha that looked more demonic than holy and near the front door hung a woman's tulle dress with pink trim. The significance was lost on him. The only thing he could think was that somehow some woman's spirit was out there hanging near the front door of the Smith house, waiting to be incarnated again into the flesh. The unknown spirit was being called back to life again, her dress waiting for her. It was an eerie sight to see that dress day after day just hanging there for all to see and ponder. What was the significance of the woman's dress hanging from a hook on the porch? He didn't know. One of the neighbors had also constructed a labyrinth in the front yard that circled the perimeters of the lawn and was marked with glass. He worried about the future generations and how they would confront that glass that was now embedded in the lawn. Too many little things worried him about his neighborhood. He needed to leave and move somewhere else where he didn't have to worry about the ever-changing, confounding, and erratic nature of those around him. He needed a fresh start with people who didn't worry him in one way or another. He needed order and not the constant worry of poverty and neglect and lack of care. His neighbors were slobs, no other way to say it. Once the neighborhood had been nice, but now it had gone to hell. And that echoed his own home environment. Everyone was too big and too old now to live in a smallish house and pretend to get along.

One person Michael wouldn't miss would be his older brother, Clemson, who went by the name Clem. Clem was the oldest and lorded it over everyone. He was twenty years old and going to the State University and majoring in agriculture although he had no desire to become a farmer or work the land. One semester he was a Philosophy major, the next an Engineer. He said he was sampling his future. And that wasn't the only thing he was sampling.

Clem had seduced their mother's helper, a timid young woman from Juárez named Lázara, who was now living in the storage shed next to the freezer. She took out her folding cot each night and went to bed with the hum of the electric appliance in her ear. It would have driven Michael crazy. His sense of hearing was too finely tuned. He could hear all sorts of fluttering, the movement of air and spirit, many things he didn't care to hear. He heard faraway and then near music at odd times of the day. Recently, he heard a man's voice in the middle of the night that talked to him from out of nowhere. He heard cats shrieking when he walked down the street and heard their distress calling out to him. He could hear plants and their growing in front of him. And one day he heard the incredible hum of the world as it breathed and gave off the freshness of its new day. Sometimes the sounds were soothing, sometimes they filled him with dread. And still, he listened. He had to, for it was his duty to bear witness to both the majesty and the terror. He knew it was his lot and sometimes it was a burden, but that's how it was. He felt so keenly aware of his life in the scheme of things. He was hyper-sensitive, and always on the yawning precipice of secrets too great to hide. Life scared him. He knew he would always be too frightened to love. For to truly love, one had to be unafraid of loss and bereavement and the eventual battering brutality of absolutely everything. He was weak and knew it. He came from frightened people who always clung to things and inculcated that sense of fear and continual dread at the loss of things. Like him, they were never free. And as a result, they were hoarders and grabbers and kept things close and familiar. One just had to peek into Lety's storage room to see the broken-down dreams of her life: antique furniture that would never be restored, a collection of vintage picture frames that would never frame any sort of images, new or old, boxes of dusty magazines that would never again be read. The room was full of damaged furniture that would never be of any use to anyone, with missing legs or pillows that would never afford any rest, with too many couches that would never support, and with tired lamps that would never shed the light on anything new. Lety had hopes but they never came to fruition. How could she create life out of the extinct vacuity of shattered dreams, a woman who could barely dress herself and shuffle out her front door?

Clem was smooth. Too smooth or so Michael thought. He whispered to too many women he shouldn't. . .comments about the way they looked, about how attractive their breasts were and so on, things they didn't want to hear, especially if they were a relative. If he wasn't related to you, maybe the women did want to hear what he had to say. But it didn't matter if the person was related or not, if he found a cousin attractive, he would approach them and mutter things under his breath. He would advance toward his prey and circle round when he knew they were least expecting it. He learned this craft from his uncles, most likely, all who were predators. From his father, Bob, he learned quiet waiting and the gift of tenacity. From his uncle Robe he learned the lazy self-absorbed manipulation of those around him. Clem would grow up to be a manipulator of women and to betray his wife countless times. He would bring his conquests to the holiday meals and to all the family gatherings, his unsuspecting wife truly clueless.

But let's not project too much at this point.

Clem was the oldest son and had decided to seduce the new girl, Lázara Domínguez. Michael had seen him go into the storage shed with the young woman who was about seventeen and recently arrived at the Stillman home. It was late at night, and everyone was asleep. Sure enough, Clem had done his whispering, and this led to his meeting Lázara in the shed. She was a young girl, alas, and Clem was a flatterer. Lázara hoped to stay in the U.S. and not go back to the poverty of her family. For whatever reasons—and some might say they were few—she loved him. At that time, there was something boyish and engaging about him. He wasn't the dissipated older man he later became. Then he was energetic and fresh and lively and hopeful. Well, hopeful he always was, but then he was young, and some might even say, charming. He came from a family of men who were able to turn a woman's head around and then walk away as she wondered what had happened. It was a family gift.

Michael followed Clem and Lázara as they entered the shed. He peered at them from a crack in the door. Lázara took off her blouse and stood in the shed facing Clem. He put his hands on her high pointy breasts and then turned her around. She faced the freezer which was near her fold-up cot with the green plastic webbing. She put her hands out in the air and then leaned them into the freezer to support herself as Clem lifted up her skirt.

Michael walked away, down the street. He hated his brother. In some sort of way, he also admired him. And later, he would emulate him as he learned to whisper and seduce his way through life. But for now, the evening was fresh, the sunset brief but beautiful as it came over the mountains. One look away and the pink gold evening light was gone and now the world was changed. What was to be done? He headed back home for his butter pecan ice cream. It was about that time.

Linda was going to meet Michael at the Arid Club. They had both been on the program for a while. It worked if it worked. Or maybe she should say: AA worked if YOU worked it. And it did work if your life didn't get in the way. Linda's life was always in the way. No matter how far away she'd gone from the street, she kept coming back, like a lemming into the sea. What exactly was a lemming? They were like eels, right?

That was her, Linda Chapa, always coming back to that small ugly home to that small ugly town to reconcile things. She hated to admit she loved Encantada and would never have left if she didn't have to. She really came to check in on her mother and see if she hadn't suffocated yet. As ever, Marielena was cheerful and self-effacing. Nothing perturbed her outwardly, and yet, like her errant daughter who never could really leave home, she was always seething inside. Someday one of them would just blow up as if they had a stick of dynamite in their heart. It was an apt metaphor as Marielena had heart problems.

As for Linda, her problems were too long of a list to enumerate. She was happy to see her old friend Michael at the AA meetings she attended daily since she'd returned home from traveling in Europe. He was a stalwart soul and somehow seeing him there with all the other "anonymous" people gave her an enormous sense of hope. No one was really anonymous in this town and so when she went to her first meeting everyone greeted her like a long-lost friend. And she was. Thank God for small, very small favors and for the grace to know that she hadn't been totally forgotten. She looked around the room and saw the same familiar faces, God love them, alcoholics all. And she was back to greet them again just where they left off, with a beer in their hearts and the taste of vodka at the back of their throats. There was no cure for what ailed them, and that knowledge gave them strength. That's not to say they were lost souls, oh no, each and every one was brave and to be commended for the willpower it took to climb that daily mountain of self-pity and sense of worthlessness. Speak for yourself, Linda Chapa.

She had started drinking secretly at age twelve with some boys at school. Don't call them friends. She had to pay for the booze in various ways, all of them degrading. Remember Sen-Sen? The breath freshener? She always smelled like Sen-Sen. It masked the booze then and the cigarette smoking which came later. She would smoke in the back yard near the neighborhood ditch by the ancient cottonwood tree and walk around afterward in the hope the smells would dissipate. She wasn't sure they ever did. But that was only one of her secrets. Somehow Chapa let her get away with it. Both knew why. Damn his soul.

The meeting was in an hour. She went out to the backyard to smoke another cigarette. She wasn't allowed to smoke inside the house. She also preferred it that way. In those early smoking days, she'd moved from Newport to Luckies, to Winston's to Marlboro's to finally the unfiltered Camels. She preferred European cigarettes like Gauloises but where were those to be found in this small town? Where was anything to be found here that mattered so much to her: bread, clothing, food, shampoo, anything de lujo, luxurious and fine? Linda had traveled all over the world but for some damn reason she kept coming home. She knew the reason why. She'd never explained it or even talked about it out loud to anyone of her many therapists. Maybe in the AA group she could bring it up. They would get it. But no, she wasn't ready yet, although she was preparing herself.

After she finished the cigarette, she walked down the street from her old house to the end and then back. Little had changed. It was still too small of a street to encompass her dreams and yet, ultimately this would be her final resting place. She knew she would never live to be an old woman. She was happy about that. Who wants to live forever? Damn forever.

How could one small street have been the place of so much suffering? How could so many children have grown up on that street that was home and afterward, when all the telling was done, no one ever wanted to call it home? Only a few of those children stayed behind. A few, like her, kept coming back to look for something lost. What had she lost here? So much. Too much. Let's start with her childhood.

Families. Separated by a yard or two or three. Each house with children, mostly girls. The year was 1966. It was a glorious, upbeat, happy, crazy-wonderful time if you were in junior high. Linda knew life awaited her, hopefully away from the small confines of her little house, her one block street, away from her controlling, domineering alcoholic father, away from her weak-willed and sometimes pathetic mother, away from the constant oppression of her father's living memory. He wasn't dead. She would have been much better off if he had been. Oh, no! Papá was very much alive with no signs of passing soon. He was short, now overweight, but he was still strong. It was her mother she worried about constantly.

The Chapas had to come up from México, for that's the path of all immigrants to this Tierra Adentro, the Interior Land. They came up the Camino Real, from México City to northern New Mexico, settling in a little town near Albuquerque. Traveling with the Oñate expedition, they arrived with the intention of conquering this land for Spain. It had been a story of conquest all along.

Linda was a history major in college, she had wanted to study law, but that slipped away with drink and drugs and finally she found her way into the travel business, where oddly enough, she excelled. As a result of her job, she had traveled all over the world and seen life in many places. Her story was not fiction and that's why it was so hard for her to share. Even at the Arid Club where nothing was left unspoken and people took your story to the grave with them, she held herself back.

Linda always wanted to go away, far away, and never come back. Well, she did go away for a while, but she always came back. And when she was away, she dreamt of home, of getting home.

She crawled through her dreams to get home. Her heart ached to be home but when she was home, she felt alone, adrift, without friends or anyone who understood her. It had been her life lesson to feel alone most of the time. And now she was beginning to see that it had also been her greatest blessing. For without solitude, rejection, discontent, rancor, and unmitigated anger at feeling so abandoned by those who should or could have been closest to her, call them kin, she wouldn't have been able to speak truth or to live the truth. The sad part of all was that she had isolated herself from those who were once her family. She wasn't invited to birthday parties. She was not on the Thanksgiving 2:00 p.m. luncheon list or the midnight Christmas eve party file. She wasn't invited to baby showers, and as a result, was never around babies. No one gave her Christmas presents or invited her over for posole or hot chocolate in the winter, and in the summer, she always found out after the fact that the party took place last week and how much fun it was. She tried to let it go and yet, it still hurt her, although she had to say, that it was probably her fault she had been shunned. She often got angry and realized she shouldn't be upset because as one relative had said to her, "You're different. We're not the same kind of people." What kind of person she was, she wasn't sure. People who speak the truth? Solitude and estrangement became her teachers.

Linda was ultimately grateful. She didn't want to be like her family: Alcoholic abusers emotionally damaged and stunted. Not kind people who never read books. People who were afraid to travel or even leave the house. People who hid behind doors and windows and lies. People who didn't share. Lazy people without volition to change the evil in their lives and those around them.

She looked hard at all the families on her street. Neighbors. Some related, some not. Children of sad fathers. Children of maimed mothers. One mother strict and harsh, one mother lax and lazy, one mother a cipher who never came out of the darkness of her house, another mother loud and brassy and often fun. They were the women who lived on her street, women who endured, and who loved the men who killed their hopes and dreams.

Her history was mostly about fathers. Or so she thought at that time. She was the legacy of the fathers' dysfunction. She couldn't pray for them, although she wanted to. Eventually all the fathers would be sent to that half-way house where dead men like them went. To a purgatory where they could be taught again to love and to become the decent men they should have always been in their lifetime—men complete in their being, with a sacred mission to be the best fathers they could be. And each one, she felt, failed. Each for different reasons. So, to them, in their life after injuring and maiming so many, including her and her sisters in suffering, her concession was to wish them well and plead with them to learn anew what it meant to be good men. There it was again: the old theme. What did it mean to be a good man, a good woman? A good mother? A good father? Fathers who shelter and love? Mothers who understand and forgive? No excuses any more for any one of them. And yet, wasn't that one of the underlying principles of AA? To forgive yourself and then others?

My name is Linda Chapa and I'm an Alcoholic.

Robert R. Stillman was born in Rodey, New Mexico. He was the son of Robert M. Stillman born in Rodey, New Mexico. His grandfather was Robert P. Stillman who was also born in Rodey.

Robert M. was a farmer and his mother, Maybelle, was a housewife. And he, Robert R., otherwise known as Robert or Bobby and then Bob Stillman, for sure didn't want to be a farmer. As soon as he could, he moved to Encantada. He got a job at the Maynard Dry Goods store on Main Street, and this is where he met Leticia Casados. The rest became their long history. Oftentimes Robert Bobby Bob thought of his grandmother, Betty Lu Ruckman, and wished that she was still in his life. She was a long-standing widow who lived with the family when he was growing up. She was a hard-of-hearing and fastidious woman of Germanic stock. Maybe because her world was so prescribed and silent, she found her outlet in the upkeep of the family home. Once Bobby and his brother Royman ate breakfast, Grandma Ruckman, or "Grammy" as she was known, would move the dining room table, sweep, and then mop the floor. This ritual was repeated every meal. Every floor surface that was mop-able was swabbed down three times daily, leading to a very clean house. Grammy Ruckman never seemed to rest unless she was locked in her little room at the back of the house and that was only during certain hours, very early and very late. Bobby had never been in her room as it was always under lock and key. And it was just as well, he had no interest in her things. He remembered her best in her 60s, 70s, and 80s when she was still a vital cleaning force in his life. She ordered the Stillman world, and everyone was grateful. Bobby knew little of his grandfather and wondered what kind of man he might have been, taking to his bed the large, imposing high-chested sow of a wife who was made to work from the moment she was born in the high plains of Colorado 'till the day she died in the desert of New Mexico. She had moved west with her husband, Robert P., to the last house she would clean on earth. That last day she finished cleaning the house, lay down in her room, and never woke up. He and his father, Robert M., had to break the door down. They found Grammy sitting up with her eyes wide open holding a well-worn Bible. She had a look of wonder and seemed very relaxed. Finally, she would have a day of rest.

Bob looked around the kitchen.

Where was Grammy when you needed her?

Devastation. Cereal boxes everywhere. Someone had left the refrigerator door slightly open. There was a trail of milk near the sink. He could hear his mother-in-law moving around in the semi-darkness. He wondered where Lety was. Had she got her mother up yet and taken her to the bathroom? Lety might be trying to sleep in like she always did and never could. Bob got up and peered into the laundry room.

Buenos Días, Adoración. He was the only one who called her by her first name. Adoration. A very old fashioned and beautiful woman's name in Spanish. So much better than Betty Lu.

¿Cómo estas? ¿Dormiste bien? Bob's Spanish was very good after living so many years with Lety's family, Adoración and her husband, Fadrique. Fadrique was like his name, a very distinguished Spaniard. He came to seek his fortune in the territory of New Mexico and ended up meeting Adoración and never returned to Salamanca where he was born. He got tired of everyone misspelling and mispronouncing his name, a version of Federico, so he went by the nickname Kiko or Kikito to those close to him. A distinguished man and tall for those around these parts, and yes, tall, for a Spaniard, he was never comfortable in his new home or with his short Mexicana wife or with all their children. Thank God their skin was more like his and unlike all their dark-skinned neighbors. It was a blessing.

Adoración mumbled something to Bubee, her son-in-law. She couldn't pronounce Bob. He was good to her, and they'd made their peace a long time ago when the upstart Cuchispete started courting her daughter, Leticia. She was against the marriage at first until she saw how he treated Lety and took care of her, so much better than the other wives of her other sons. What did it matter if he was a Gringo? Kikito was a Spaniard and that was more bothersome. If she had a consejo, and she had many, it was to think twice about marrying someone from Spain.

Bob came up to his mother-in-law to see how she was faring. No doubt she needed a diaper change. He would tend to that shortly. But first he would get her oatmeal going. She needed a good breakfast. He would get her up, take her to the bathroom in her wheelchair, and then bring her back to her room to change her clothing and put on a clean diaper. Then he'd wheel her into the kitchen, and they would have oatmeal together. It was their daily ritual. Everyone was asleep or pretending to be asleep, and the house was quiet and momentarily peaceful.

Adoración would be set for a while, at least until Lety got up and started moving around.

Bob put in a large load of laundry. Soon it would be time to get to work at the car dealership. He had some call backs to check up on. The sales had been poor the last few months and he was worried. He might have to borrow some money from his brother-in-law, Randy, the accountant businessman who had done well for himself. He dreaded that. No, he'd have to hustle again somehow. How he dreaded approaching anyone for a loan, most of all his well-off brother-in-law who was always willing to loan him money and help in any way he could, the son of a bitch.

Bob rarely cursed although he felt he had many reasons to do so.

Adoración liked her café in the morning with lots of milk. And so did Bubee. They never spoke much at breakfast or at any other time, but somehow it was comforting and pleasant to sit in that humid kitchen, the window slightly misted with the early morning cold and ponder the new day, the fresh day, its opportunities, its hope.

Lety came in from watering the yard. There wasn't much to water, but she did what she could. There was that big tree near the street and those trees to the side near the kitchen. The yard—no yard. Not much to water and yet she would head out first thing in the morning to see how things were going in the world. The tree was dying, let's start there.

It had been hard to get up. All she wanted to do was sleep. When would that day come when she could sleep without having to worry about so many other people? She had to lay down and think about that.

She felt tired. No reason other than a tiredness of tired times. A tired without remedy. That kind of tired. Best to lay down while the house was quiet, the kids in school, Mamá sleeping in her room. The washing machine quiet. It was a good time to rest. Supper? Too tired to think about it. Maybe her spaghetti. Maybe enchiladas. Maybe quesadillas. Something fast. What would that be? Cereal? Hot or cold?

There were good times on Encantada Street. When Vicky turned six, Mundo got a very large piñata in Juárez and set it up in the backyard. It was hell to rig up as there was nothing to tie it to, but he finally got it up by attaching it to the roof, rasquache Mexican style. All the children in the neighborhood were invited to the party, and that included all the cousins and their parents. The adults had drinks in the house with a huge meal of tacos, beans, and rice. The children sat outside at a table, with chaperones, of course, and ate peanut butter and banana sandwiches. There was a huge fruit punch bowl in the dining room and on the table was a large chocolate cake surrounded by biscochos and party mints. The party went on until it got dark and many of the children were taken home. The women left with their charges and some of the neighborhood men came back to have more drinks. Joe Blanco and his wife, Senaida, returned and so did Lety and Bob Stillman. Mundo wasn't too happy about Joe coming back as he was a hard drinker and unpleasant when he got drunk. Fortunately, he and Senaida got into a huge fight, and they walked home, which was just down the street. But dammit, you could hear them long into the night. Bob and Lety left shortly afterward. Mundo sat in the backyard with the piñata shards, the candy cleaned out earlier by the children. They'd had a good time and Vicky was so happy. She was his consentida, his spoiled baby girl. He loved her then and still loved her now. She was his baby girl and that's something special for a man. It's probably good he didn't have any sons. He didn't know how they would turn out. With girls, there was some hope. Girls had a sign of benediction on their foreheads and their lives were somehow better, at least in his family.

He felt a pain in his stomach. What was going on? He'd had the pain for weeks now and probably should tell Vicky about it. It was like someone had punched him in the stomach, right under the breastbone.

Mundo saw too many doctors now. It was an old man's fate. He never thought he'd live so long. If he had known, he would have taken better care of himself. Now it was too late. His mother lived to be a hundred, over a hundred. No one knew how old Paquita Fuentes was. When you asked her how old she was, she would say fifty. Somehow, she'd gotten stuck at that age. He remembered fifty. That's when things started happening with his body. He began to have trouble swallowing, and sometimes he felt dizzy and thought he might pass out. He'd stopped drinking for a while and things would get better. Eventually he'd go back to his old haunts for he missed his drinking life. It was his special life, a life he needed, a life he loved.

Around that time, he found out he was a diabetic. He started on the pills, and it helped for some time. But gradually, the diabetes began to wear him down and he had to give himself shots. This was around the time he decided to move back home. He and Erme had divorced the year after Vicky's piñata party, and he'd moved to the other side of town. But it wasn't enough. Erme would follow him or show up at the post office where he worked, and she would make a scene. She was the dramatic one! Crying and begging him to come home for Vicky's sake. He made the mistake of going back and that's when Clarita was conceived. And so, he did go back, for a time. And then he left and stayed gone except when he came back which was too often. Erme would give him his shots and feed him lunch and then he'd go back to work and sometimes he stayed over, and it would begin all over again. He could never really leave. That was the problem with everyone who lived on that street. They wanted to leave, but they never really could. Look at poor Chapa! Look at that fool Stillman with his wife! Look at Joe Blanco! All of them fools without a will. And he was the same. Maybe it was something in the water. It *was* full of lithium. It deadened you and made you docile. Or worse, it made you think things would work out when there was never hope from the day your compadre put the lazo around your neck and the priest pronounced you husband and wife. That traditional wedding cord was there to choke you and hold you back from the world. Mundo had wanted to travel far, and he did get out of town during the war when he joined the army. It was a brief respite for him and gave him a taste of the world. He was stationed in New York, and he saw what life was like on the East Coast. He liked the anonymity of the crowds and the rush and pull of city life. But it wasn't to last. His father, Nicanor became ill, and he came home to hear his father's last words and see him flutter like a moth to his flaming death. His mother, Paquita, was beside herself and he decided to help her out. But she drove him crazy and by then, he was already in the drinking life. He moved out to an apartment near the post office. He met Ermelinda, or Erme, as he called her when he was feeling loving, at a birthday party for his cousin. The rest is the rest. He remembered that birthday party. Erme was very elegant and was more refined that the other woman he'd known in Encantada. She had gone to school with some Mexican nuns and knew the ways of society. Once, she had thought of becoming a nun herself, but she said it wasn't the life for her. And, for sure, Ermelinda Castellón was a beautiful woman. Just like Vicky. Look at Erme and you will see their daughter. And Vicky, well, he remembered her at that birthday party so many years ago. A sweet little girl with long brown hair with golden highlights. You don't often see that color of hair. It was brown, yes, but it was a rich root beer brown like her eyes. They were deep set like Erme's. People say that the eyes are the entrance to the soul. It was a corny thought, but he liked it. More than once he had looked into Erme's eyes and knew that although he loved her, he would one day leave her. She was too possessive. She wouldn't let him breathe.

The piñata bounced high and then low. It dipped and swayed and with each movement, there were cries of joy. He remembered the way the children screamed with happiness. He remembered the bright and precious face of his little girl. And in the background was Erme, beautiful and distant, both shining stars in his galaxy of dreams. He wanted more for them. And for himself? He just wanted to be left alone. No more screaming and yelling and telling him to stop, stop, stop!

Can't you stop, Mundo, can't you stop drinking? You're ruining your family and here I am now with a baby on the way. Look at me.

I am.

Don't you care? Tell me you care.

I did care. But everything was bigger than the explanations I could ever give you. Didn't you know? You wanted answers. I couldn't give you answers. It just didn't work out. Someday I'll answer you. But not now, Erme. Not now.

Lety had so many reasons. Bobby never learned how to dance. Even now, after all these years he still did that same lame goose step that simulated rhythm. Lety had loved to dance and was what some called the life of the party. She was irreverent, funny, caustic, and witty, like everyone else in her family. They were funny people with everyone except themselves. Cruelty to each other was rife. They couldn't help it. They grew up bitter. It came from their mother. She was a cold and unsympathetic person. And she was a bad cook to boot. All her children spoke of her deprecatingly. They had reason to. She wasn't there when she should have been. She favored one son, neglecting all the others.

Lety wanted to dance the way she once had. But now she used a cane. The weakness came on slowly at first and then it took over. Her steps were halting. She over-compensated and soon she, too, had some sort of goose step and she hated that. She had once been young, once been limber. Now she was dying. Few people came to see her anymore. She was rail thin, emaciated beyond belief. She looked like a survivor from some terrible war, someone who hadn't eaten in a long time. She couldn't eat. Everything became sour in her stomach and what she had once loved became poison to her. No red chile, no more ice cream, no more sodas, no more no more. She ate soups now, and hot oatmeal thinned out or grits or atole, some kind of watery gruel to give her strength.

There were many reasons. She should have had a better life, a more comfortable life instead of the one she had. It had been too much of a struggle. Bobby never made a good living and after they married, she couldn't work. She had wanted to, but there were the children, her mother Adoración. Mamá became her life and her cross and maybe her redemption. If she did go to Heaven, which she doubted, it would be because she had taken care of her mother for over forty years. The lost years. The same number of years the Israelis wandered the desert looking for the Promised Land.

Her bedroom was dark, and she wanted to call out, but her voice was weak. When had it disappeared? She used to tell jokes, had great stories, could have been a comedian, yes, she was that funny. Now she had a mouth full of dust.

Take me to the living room she wanted to tell her daughter. All the children had disappeared. Adelaida? No, it wasn't Adelaida. It was another woman. Who was she? The sons were all cowards. They couldn't stand to see her weighing sixty pounds. Sixty pounds of blood and pus. Sixty pounds of rage and ugliness. The nieces and nephews stayed away. When she saw them, she insulted them and made them feel bad. Where have you been? Why haven't you come to see me? What do you see? A living skeleton? Go on, look at me. How does it feel to see a dead woman? How does that make you feel?

No one wanted her rage to touch them. They stayed away. She was the woman who made snide remarks, the one who criticized, the one who gossiped and the one who made you feel bad because you didn't love her enough. You had loved her once, found her warm and special. You were once friends, but now you just wanted to get away from her.

She had her reasons. She was always poor when she should have been rich. She should have had a lovely home, but it was always messy. She couldn't afford help and when she did, the help helped others, never her. The help was poor girls from México who never stayed long. They always left after a week or two and never recommended anyone to take over their jobs. One of them told her to her face that she worked them too hard. And not only that, but that her sons were mujeriegos and that they were a disgraceful bunch of lecherous men. They had tried to touch her and get her to do things with them. The last girl that had worked for her told worse things. Lety didn't believe them at first. The girl accused one of the sons of trying to rape her. That's the kind of sons you have. Right then and there she asked the girl to leave and threw her clothing out the door. Liar. She was a liar.

Her brothers were that way, but not her sons. It wasn't true. It wasn't true her sons had turned out like their uncles. She didn't want to think about it. The girl had provoked her sons, that was it. She was a whore. They were all whores.

It was true one of her daughters had several children out of wedlock. She and Bobby had sent her away, but then she came back and got pregnant again. There was no help for her. How did she become that kind of person? And yet it was that daughter who was helping take care of Lety. That one. She was the one who cleaned her and wiped her when she bled down there and flowed that dark black stew of blood and fecal matter. It was she who fed her the watery gruel that kept her alive for the short while she was still able to eat.

Now Lety couldn't eat and yes, she had her reasons. She had tried to be a good mother and she wasn't. Her children did love her, but not fully. She was cold like her mother, Adoración. It couldn't be helped. She carried the hardness in her genes. She wasn't fully capable of loving. She and her brothers didn't know what real love was. And yet. . .there was Bobby. There was that time when she was special and alive and full of joy. She wanted to earn a college degree, become a professional woman, have a nice home and land to build on. She had wanted those things that were never granted her.

She had her reasons. There were many. They were profound reasons and they outweighed whatever good came her way. No reason to struggle with it anymore. No reason to say yes or no or maybe so. Mamá was gone now. After all those years of hard work and her being the sad- barely-breathing part of the house. She was gone suddenly without hardly an intake of air. After all the time of uncertainty and struggle. Children leave and don't visit. Daughters find ways to shame, and sons become enemies. So do other relatives. Some of them you talk to and some of them you don't. The ones you dislike avoid you and you them. You chalk it up to their personalities and their unforgiving ways but really, it was you who was the unlikeable and unlovable one. You had your reasons.

You tried to protect yourself. You wanted the best for your family. You tried to give your children hope. But you had so little yourself. You just got tired. Everything became that living organism inside of you that wanted to scream.

You had your reasons. No one understood. If they did, they turned away when you started to tell them why. No one listened.

How would they know? Yes, you were bitter. You had your reasons. There was too much disappointment. Too much worry. Too much lack. Too much disorder. Everyone clamoring. The inside of you got lost. You never danced again the way you had danced before. With abandon and with joy. Those days were long gone. Those days were a faraway past of longing for what would never be. Sorrowful and distant, that was you. Still is you. You have your reasons. No one to listen to you except those few. If even. God disappeared. He stepped outside. He went out the back door and slammed it shut. He walked away down that damned little street and didn't look back. He declared bankruptcy and left you without a dime. The dime was never yours. The dime was borrowed. It should have been yours, but it wasn't. It belonged to someone else. And you knew it. Bobby knew it. Your children knew it, all of them. They lived a secondhand life. They were impostors. All of them faking it. All of them pretending to love. You had your reasons. And they knew it. They had their reasons, and you knew why. It's a good thing you won't live to see it. It would probably be disappointment. What else? I could go on and on. I wanted to say so many things to so many people. I held back when I should have spoken. I spoke when I should have held back. I was hard and there was a reason. My people were difficult and unforgiving and unloving and cold. And yet, I remember. I do remember sometimes that Mamá held me close. Most of the time she was so distant. She couldn't help herself. She had such a hard time. Her father would go away, wander off, just like all the men in this family, well, except for Bobby, they'd just flat out disappear, and when you needed them, they would be gone, just like that. Those were my brothers. My uncles. My father. And my sisters, well they were rich or dead. We had to stay alive because it was unthinkable to give up just like that. We had our reasons. We were proud people who had nothing and deserved more. We came from people who once had much. Once owned. Once loved. Now we were bereft. What happened? Who was the woman who cursed us and brought down the vengeance to our family? She was in the past of us. She had her reasons. And that man? Who was he? Our great-great grandfather? The one who began it all. How was it we lost our way? Who cursed us and brought us shame? And why? They had their reasons. Who and what they were I don't know, will never know. I do know this. They had their reasons.

It was raining. Lety could hear the drops outside her window. It was late and still she couldn't sleep. There was much to be reconciled. The dead wanted to talk to her and explain what they could. She tried to listen. They had so much to say, and one would think in an eternity of time they would have composed the words. But no. They had their reasons. The dead don't speak with their mouths. Their mouths are full of dust. Their eyes speak and sometimes the eyes of the dead aren't the eyes of those you once loved. Other people come to inhabit the forms of those you once loved, tried to love. They appear and then disappear, and you never know when they are speaking truth and if they are the people they pretend to be. After a while you do discern that the person in front of you is not the person in front of you but someone else. Evil has a way of masking. It is clever. It manipulates emotion. It takes advantage of longing. It deceives. But you continue to outrun the darkness and after a while, the door closes and the spirit tires and goes away because it has been discovered to be a lie. It almost seems too late or nearly too late.

Lety wanted to call out to someone, but nothing came out of her mouth. It was dry. The spirits were talking to her again.

Today's the day. This is the moment. Listen.

The dead were coming back to tell her secrets.

I'm listening.

Are you? You still want me to talk? This is only the beginning of the story. This story is incomplete, but that's the way it is. Tomorrow is another day. And the story isn't the one I thought I would be telling you. Within me moves a great sadness for you. I'm so sorry. Instead of horror I feel pity.

I can't hear you. I hear the rain.

The rain?

Oh. Now it's stopped.

Joe Blanco was a good catch. Everyone in town thought so. He was tall, handsome, perhaps a little too thin, but that would be remedied in time. Senaida would take care of him and fatten him up a little. Nothing she couldn't handle. She wasn't a good cook, but she would learn how to cook for him. There wasn't anything she wouldn't give to say that Joe Blanco was her boyfriend. He came from the Blanco family, and they were good-looking men. She chased after him like any smart forward-looking young woman would do. Joe Blanco wasn't only boyfriend material; he was husband material. Senaida pursued him as only she could. When she put her mind to something, nothing could stop her. She was a stubborn woman and came from people who never let go. She came from old stock, true stock, from Native people who knew the land, worked it, and never gave up. Her father was a cotton farmer, and her mother was a schoolteacher. Both taught Senaida that any success in life came first from the power of will. She made up her mind that Joe Blanco would become her husband.

There was something lively and brassy and breathless about Senaida when she was young. She wasn't beautiful; she was a large-boned woman with big hips and small breasts, but she had something other woman lacked—extreme self-confidence. She had a passion to see things through. She'd studied to be a stenographer, and no one could beat her at dictation or typing. She'd won contests for her typing and shorthand skills. Nowadays did anyone do shorthand anymore? She planned on becoming an Administrative Secretary and then the business manager of an office and then the Director and then who knows? She was set to be a successful businesswoman who was highly paid. She had it planned out. Once she married Joe, they would move out of town to a large city back East.

Oh, she would be happy to leave Encantada behind. The only person she would miss would be her widowed mother. But she would visit her often and later, send for her, and her mother would live with them. Joe would get a high paying job doing what he loved best. He was studying to be a Civil Engineer. She wasn't exactly sure what Civil Engineers did, but whatever they did, they got paid well. They wouldn't have children for a while, and then when they were ready, they would have two children, a boy, and a girl. Senaida had it all planned out. Encantada was a small town, and it could never encompass her dreams. She wanted more that her hometown could offer. It was all planned out.

Nothing happened the way Senaida Roybal planned. She got pregnant and she and Joe had to get married fast. That was how it was done in those days. The wedding wasn't much, most of the people in attendance were family. She'd wanted a large wedding with half of Encantada there, but the reception was a dismal affair at the Knights of Columbus Hall. First, they got married at City Hall and later, after the baby was born, they got married in church although the priest wasn't too happy about it. Fortunately, he didn't know them and had just moved into town. They paid him a little extra and it was a done deal. She didn't wear a long gown as she'd wished but a white suit instead. She'd gained a lot of weight with Joe Jr., and it showed. It was the beginning of her weight gain. It was around that time that the truth became apparent. It happened on their wedding night, right after the Civil ceremony. Joe got drunk and roughed her up. Then he took off and she didn't see him until the next morning when he sheepishly showed up at her mother's house. They were looking for an apartment and had decided to stay with her mother for a while to save money. Mrs. Roybal was so angry at Joe that she barred him from entering the house and Senaida had to go outside and meet him. They moved into a motel that night and it took months for her mother to forgive him. Mrs. Roybal never did like Joe after that, not that she had liked him before. Their friendship was doomed.

As far as the newlyweds were concerned, their relationship went from all right to bad to very bad to unacceptable. Three children later, they slept in separate bedrooms in the same house, ate at different hours, had their own distinctive schedules, and had their own friends. They had little in common other than their children. The children never got along with each other or their parents. It was a mess all around. Senaida never finished her degree and became a stay-at-home mom who worked Shaklee part time or Mary Kay or whatever else was in fashion. Joe never finished his Engineering Degree. He took a job in the Motor Vehicle Department and eventually, by default, because no one else wanted the job, he became the Manager.

The Blanco's moved to Encantada Street right after their son was born.

What happened to the finer things in life, Senaida wondered? Art? Literature? Where was culture in all of this? Senaida read pulp novels and recommended her favorite book to her neighbor, Linda Chapa. It was called The Sun Also Rises. A good title. The book? A synopsis goes as follows: Setting: early days of an American settlement. Part of the book is set in England. A young and handsome sea captain travels the world. He has a virginal fiancée back in England who is lily white, as only a purebred English woman can be. She was waiting for him to return to her so they could marry. She was pining for him and vice versa. But not really. The Englishman, on one of his trips, stopped on a remote island or country, the details escaped her, to gather slaves. He met up with a beautiful young black slave. Senaida couldn't remember her name, guess it was time for her to read the book again! He became obsessed with the woman and hid her below deck. She was his captive. She became the wild fruit of his hidden desires and deprived him of all dignity, protocol, and decency. What happened at the end of the book? Did the virginal princess win out and marry the handsome but reckless captain and move to the States, or did he return to the world of the heathen goddess he has come to love? His was not love, but madness. At any rate, the book illustrated that most men and women must confront that lunacy in their lives that allows them to do foolish things in the heat of passion. The thing was to see it. Live it. Move on.

Senaida loved the book. She knew Linda was back again to visit her parents and probably needed a good book. She saw her passing through the yard of the shadowy shuttered house and stopped her, book in hand.

Linda! How are you? It's Senaida. It's Sen. Are you back?

Senaida knew Linda wouldn't stay too long. She never did. Might as well get some good reading in. Something to pass the time.

Linda didn't look too good. She was young and yes, beautiful with a trim and lovely body but she always seemed so sad. Her eyes were red, and Senaida figured she'd been crying. She had bags under her eyes as well and her skin looked mottled. What was going on?

You okay, Linda?

How you been, Sen?

Oh, me? The usual. How could I be? Nothing much changes. How's Joe?

Him? He's in his office. That's what I call his car.

I thought I saw him.

Yeah, he's reading the newspaper in there. He does it every day. Not that I care.

I have to go now, Sen. I'll be late for my meeting.

Oh yeah? Well, I was thinking of you. I ran across this book and wondered if you wanted to read it. It's probably my favorite book of all time.

I'll have a look. Catch you tomorrow, okay? I'm running late. I have a meeting.

Sure. Sure Linda. Sure.

Say hello to your Mama. I never see her.

Say hello to Joe.

Hell, I never see him. I mean it, we live in the same house, but you know, he has his side and I have mine. That's how it is.

I'm sorry.

Don't be. We like it that way.

Why don't you move out?

And let him have the house? Hell, no! I worked too hard for that damn house. He can move out. But he won't. So, there you have it. Him on one side, me on the other. It's a good thing the kids are gone. Well, except Sandy, but she mostly stays with her boyfriend. Not that I like that, but you know. Kids. Nowadays people shack up. Kids. You have someone? I mean I don't want to be nosey. You coming back and all. Just wondered.

I'm not staying long. I came back to see my mother.

You staying with her?

I have an apartment now.

Oh yeah?

Here's the book.

Tomorrow.

What's it called?

The Sun Also Rises.

Oh, okay.

It's gripping.

Just what I need, Sen. Something gripping.

You take care.

YOU take care, Sen. You got to move out.

Hell, no. And lose my claim on the house? Hell, no. Wave to Joe when you go by. He's out there in his office. Son of a bitch.

Mundo sat in his chair. The maid had just cleared away his dinner. The food was all right whatever it was. He couldn't remember what it was, but it was all right. He might need to go to the bathroom. He felt his lower abdomen. No. Not yet. He wasn't ready to call the woman yet. She would help walk him to the bathroom with his walker and then get him ready for bed. But it still wasn't time.

Maybe Vicky would come over. He hadn't seen her in a few days. Or was it yesterday? He couldn't remember. He would ask the woman. No, he wouldn't. She was all right this one, not like the last one Vicky hired. He didn't want to think about her. And before it was that man. He didn't like him one bit. Vicky should have known better. He didn't want no joto helping him out. No way. Mundo didn't want no mano doblada helping him with anything. Vicky should have known better.

Mundo looked out the large picture window in the living room. Vicky said it was his house. He didn't remember buying it. He'd never had a house. He always rented. Except when he lived here a long time ago, when Erme was alive. She'd been dead now a while. How long? It seemed like yesterday. That was shortly after he moved back to Encantada Street. Maybe a year later. When was that? He couldn't remember. How long ago was that? It seemed like only yesterday Erme was here and then she was gone.

He called her one night and said I'm coming home.

What?

I mean I'm coming back, but not to live with you.

Oh. You're coming back?

Home, but not home. I'll need to find a place to live. Can you help me?

He didn't remember her response. Divorced over thirty years and he was still asking for her help. That's how it was. Probably how it would always be. Dammit!

Erme helped him find this place. Vicky said it was his house. How can it be his house? He didn't remember buying it.

Erme helped clean it, put up curtains, and had a group of women paint the rooms. She always had those sorts of women around her to help her. Sure enough, Erme had it ready for him when he came back to town. It was nice, very nice. The only problem was that it was down the street from his old house, their house, on the same street. Nothing to be done, he thought. At least I have my own house. It was a good house with two bedrooms. Erme fixed it up just fine, added her touch to all things: curtains, tablecloths, towels, furniture, and dishes. It was lacking nothing. She did all that for him. He was grateful. And then she died.

But before she got the cancer that killed her so fast, he remembered how she would come over with food for him. Or she would invite him over to eat. He never lacked food. Maybe it wasn't such a bad thing to move back. His favorite bar was nearby; he could walk if he wanted to. And sometimes he did walk there and back home. Sometimes he forgot where his car was when he'd walked over, or the car wasn't there, and he thought it was. He got confused, especially after the last call.

He dreamt he was looking for his car and he couldn't remember where he left it. He was often lost in a strange city looking for his car or his apartment. The dreams varied. And sometimes he might have missed seeing his car because he forgot what his car looked like. And then sometimes he remembered he didn't have a car, and that he was looking in vain. Or if he got to his apartment or his hotel room, he couldn't remember the number of the room. Sometimes he didn't have the key. And sometimes when he did get to his room, there were strangers inside. Oftentimes he tried to get to the airport and was late. His suitcase wasn't packed, or he couldn't take all the things he wanted to take. He would look around the room and wonder what was important and what he could leave behind. He was always running late. If he couldn't find the car, how could he get to the airport? He had so much clothing, so many things, many that mattered to him. How would he decide what to leave behind? He was always trying to leave and never getting there. He just knew he had to get somewhere. And soon. Oftentimes he was on a plane. He didn't like flying. And if he was driving, he was always going too fast and about to go over some precipice. He was always afraid. Every night it was another adventure. He was exhausted.

He remembered the good times with Erme at the end of what should have been the beginning of their getting along after all the years of being apart. She was a good woman when she wanted to be, and now she was so much better than he remembered. All those prayer meetings had done some good. Sometimes he felt sad when he looked at her, still a beautiful woman with her fine high cheek bones, those dark brown deep-set eyes, her formidable and still attractive body. What he didn't like was the usual: her nagging him about the Drink. The Drink.

When are you going to stop, Mundo? Look at you!

He didn't have to look in the mirror to see what he looked like now. Splotchy face, a small body with weak legs and thin arms. A constant cough and the worst problem: a throat that would close and cause him to choke. Too much acid, the doctor said. He had to start going in to get his throat opened. Varying sizes of metal tubes were put down his throat to open it up—it was like having crabgrass in his esophagus. It was an ugly thing to think about—a thin tube, then a thicker tube and so on, until the thickest tube moved down his throat like a reluctant serpent seeking its way through a swamp. This is what the Drink did to him. It closed his throat. It made him choke. And he almost died several times. It was terrible when he couldn't eat and was afraid to choke. Or he ate and never knew if he could swallow the food, whatever it was. After a while he started buying cans of baby food. It was terrifying. That's when he called Erme.

I'm coming home.

What?

I mean I'm coming back, but not to live with you.

Oh. You're coming back?

Home, but not home.

I'll need to find a place to live. Can you help me?

Can you help me, Ermelinda? Can you help me? Can you give me some of your strength? I need it now, Erme. I'm afraid. I'm not sure what is happening. I don't want to die, not yet Erme. Not yet. I'm still young. What is it you always say, I may be old, but I'm not a viejita, there's a difference. I'm not a viejito, Erme. But I'm afraid. Can you help me? We had some happy times. When Vicky was a little girl. Remember that time I rigged up the piñata for her birthday? How old was she? What year was that?

Don't be sad anymore about what happened between us. It couldn't be helped. We were so different. I tried. I know you tried. You tried more than I tried. But we were so different. I don't think I ever told you how many times I just wanted to get in the car and drive back home. I would dream about coming back. I could see the house and it looked the same but different. I was always trying to get home. But I couldn't find the car, or I was in a strange city, or I couldn't find my suitcase or my keys or I was late for the plane and then I would wake up. It had all been a bad dream. I would go back to sleep thinking of you, Erme. Hoping and knowing you were praying for me. Otherwise, I don't think I could have made it.

Turns out it was a pretty good book if you like books that go on for a thousand pages, span generations, are set in England, the fledgling U.S colonies, Barbados, but not in that order. It was a great book if you ponder the themes of love, lust, and passion. Although the slavery part was very disturbing.

In a way, the protagonist, Matthew Flood, wasn't so different from the men on Encantada Street. What were they anyway, but holdovers from a feudal backward Macho society that still believed that women should be their slaves. Many of them were Mama's boys who were spoiled by their mothers, and who were slaves to their fathers.

There was Linda's father, Rafael, their neighbor, Joe, and from what she'd heard, Mundo down the street. The viejito was still riding roughshod over his daughter, Victoria. The old man was still yelling and carrying on even though he couldn't walk a straight line, any line, or down the street unaided. And that street had once been his kingdom. It was the kind of street where no one walked on the sidewalks. Everyone was known to walk the middle of the street at all times of the day and night, flaunting and challenging the cars that occasionally drove by. And if someone was brave enough and rude enough to drive by, the residents of the street followed them with a hard gaze and a shout out to slow down, SLOW DOWN, CABRÓN! People were always trying to drive fast on the little street. The worst offender was a teenage boy that lived at the end of the street, all bad skin, and spindly legs. He was always peeling down from one end to another without regard for life, animal, or human. Petey was a terror and the sooner he went off to college or the army or hell, the better off the neighborhood would be.

In certain ways, all the men on the street ruled their families, would always rule them.

And who ruled these men? The demons: alcohol, pride, the belief in control, and their twisted sex lives that lived behind the walls of the street's houses. They were all weak, contaminated men. For whatever reasons, they had all been polluted, and in their desire to be in control of whatever was out of control in them, and so much was, they victimized those closest to them.

Linda hated her father for abusing her.

She hated it when he came into her bedroom when she was a young girl, still unformed mentally but with the body of someone much older. He entered her room in the early morning when her mother, Mariaelena, was still asleep.

Couldn't her mother hear him? Couldn't she feel him leave her bed—she who guarded the street so ferociously and who knew who came and went? She may not have been outside watching the comings and goings of those who dared cross her street, but she was one of those who peered from closed curtains, turned aside many times in each very long day. She knew the bark of each dog on the street, knew their distinctive growls and knew the cries of various cats in heat, any animals in pain. She heard the family of skunks come and go and she saw the raccoons that lived in the alley hidden away in daylight. Once she saw a fox run down the street and yes, the crows were counted and known.

Why couldn't she hear Rafael go into her daughter's room, hear her muffled cries, and recognize the sound of him struggling and straining to remove her clothes and then relieve himself on her? Was she asleep all those times or only pretend sleeping? It was a small house, a house that pinged and breathed and perspired in the heat and shivered in the cold. It was a house like all the houses on the street: small, with only one bathroom, usually two or sometimes three bedrooms, a small living room, a small kitchen and a small hallway that divided the adults from the children.

Why didn't anyone hear what was going on? Where was her mother? Where were her sisters? Where was her brother? Where were the neighbors? Their walls were thin and sometimes after Rafael left her shivering with fear, or feverish with nausea, she could hear the neighbors talking to each other, or calling for their animals to come in, come home, or maybe she just imagined she heard voices outside. Maybe she wanted them to look in her window and see what was happening inside. She wanted to see someone's face out there in the darkness. A woman's face. She wanted to hear someone's shriek saying stop. Stop. Stop! Stop!

In a faraway dream Linda remembered someone putting something inside her body. Something cold and sharp. What was it?

Years later, when she had gone and come back and gone again and once again returned, Linda wondered if there wasn't something evil going on in the neighborhood. Did the men share their lusts and desires with each other? Did they share their children, their stories? Were they part of a sick and secret club? What they did to their children was unspeakable.

She was afraid to find out too much. And still, she wondered. . .

She could never speak to anyone about it. She did bring it up with her group. No one said anything. They just listened. No one seemed perturbed. It was as if what she was talking about was something they all knew about. No one judged her or seemed shocked or disgusted. What everyone had lived through made them immune to poison it seemed. They had been bitten by rattlers and lived to tell the story. It was a relief and still the burden hung on. She would re-live again and again the story all her life. What was left of her life? She knew she wouldn't live to be a grandmother. She never wanted to marry, never wanted children. She knew too much. And to know too much in a small town is to call out banishment.

Later, she would learn about certain families in her town. How they did rituals and belonged to cults and did things horrible, secret, and dark. There was a colony of them in the valley. She had heard about the group from several people and when they talked about the dark people they spoke in whispers. How can you even suggest it her mother Marielena said one time when Linda tried to confront her about the brujas and what they did. Mi'ija, what are you talking about? Don't mention it again. I forbid you. And then she crossed herself three times in the name of the Father, Son and Holy Ghost followed by a kiss to the lips.

Marielena wasn't a particularly spiritual person. She had stopped going to Mass when she married Rafa. Maybe if she had kept on going to Mass, Linda thought, maybe then her faith would have protected them.

The people that were evil were people everyone knew about. They were in her family and her neighbor's families. They lived in town and outside of town. They were Anglo and they were Mexicanos. Most were rich and very few were poor. Evil likes the good life.

She remembered things being done to her. She remembered a cold metal object. What was it? And she remembered someone sticking a candle in her opening. Why would anyone put wax in a child's little sex? It had been so uncomfortable and so strange. Candles were what you lit in church when you talked to God. And God answered back in the cool of the holy place. I am your Lord and Savior.

Now it was too late. No one would believe her, ever if she spoke of the things that had been done to her. Not only in her room, but in other places, down the street and what seemed far away. Sometimes her father would take her with him, and they would go see his friends. She hated going with him, but she had no choice. Her mother never left the house so what would she know about the men and what they did to her?

No one wanted to know too much in the small town. Underneath the veneer lived the dark people who spent their time in the festering and hidden darkness of power and control. She could give you names now that she was older. She remembered faces. She could never forget the small dark face of the little Spanish priest or the man who worked at the bank. She thought about the principal of the elementary school and the woman who was the nurse. But no one would believe her. And why should they? They were monied, upstanding, well-known, and yes, respected people. They were president of this and manager of that. And the women were even sometimes worse than the men. She never knew then that women could be so cruel. And sometimes they were worse than the men. Witches, all of them.

She wasn't making this up. She had to go away to begin to understand what the truth was. The truth was that her little town was evil. Her family was no family. Her father was not a father. Her mother was a victim. And she, oh, she was so tired of everything!

She had tried to kill herself several times. Pills. Later she preferred the slow death by alcohol. And now that she was sober what was she going to do? How would it work out? She had saved up money from those years of travel and work, and now she just wanted to rest a little. She'd come home for the quiet afternoons in the early Fall when it was warm, and she sat outside and smoked a cigarette. She didn't need much but the quiet and an occasional breeze. The smell of comino and chile filled the air. The harvest was over, and it had been good. The sack of cebollas hung in the garage of her mother's house. The costal of chile was alongside. Red enchiladas with onion. Her favorite food. This is what home was about. It was about things she loved. The intermittent whistle of the train going north. The lumbering sound of metal on metal. The slow, languorous, and soft summer night when things cooled down. Walking around the neighborhood just to see what was going on and what was new. What was new? Nothing much. Nothing at all. Things were still beautiful to her, despite everything. This time she wouldn't leave. She would stay. My name is Linda, and I am a warrior.

Michael had memories of spending too much time splayed out on one of the long living room couches that his mother favored, wondering what he was going to do. The couches were longer then. You needed a long couch for so many people. The couches were crème colored, beige, brown, the colors never varied much. They never had a white couch. The colors of everything in the house were similar: brown and browner. It would have been nice to have a bright red or dark blue couch. Something with a pattern. Beige was a good color to hide dust and dirt. Not that their house was dirty, it was more messy, full of boxes and clothing strewn around here and there. His mother was always going to sales at discount stores, and so when she found a good buy everyone got the same outfit. The girls hated this, and the boys didn't care.

He spent hours on the couch daydreaming. This occurred mostly at night when everyone else was asleep. He would slip out of his room and maybe go for a walk in the cool darkness and make his way through the neighborhood. He had various routes: to the park and back, to downtown and back, around the back way. He varied the route as he wished. And he was never tired of walking, especially late at night when his family and the town were asleep. He would return to the quiet house and lie on a couch in the living room or the room where they had the first black and white television on the street and think. Just think. What was he going to do?

Michael was long. He had long feet and long arms and a long torso. Even though the couches were long, they were always too small for him and too short.

Sometime his uncle Robe would stay with them when he came into town and would sleep on the couch in the television room. He said he didn't want to be in the way, but he was. How could he think of staying with them when he had a perfectly good apartment up North? Robe said he got lonely for family. It was odd because he never seemed to care much for anyone except when he got into one of his melancholic moods every few months and insisted on staying with them so he could visit his mother, Adoración.

When Robe came into town, he displaced everyone. He was an estorbo, a bother. Although when Robe was there everyone seemed a little happier. He was a funny man and had them laughing all the time. The family would spend the evenings eating ice cream and sitting on one or another long beige couch as they listened to Robe go on with his stories. His mother seemed to come alive and joined in the bad jokes, the critical and brash commentary and soon, everyone was laughing. They were a good comedy team and could have performed in public. Ice cream would be served and then everyone would quiet down. Robe would leave for a while and everyone knew he was headed to the bar down the road, close to Main Street. Its name was a misnomer: The Happy Lounge. As far as things went, no one was ever happy in that place. It was dark and smelled of booze and sadness. Can sadness have a smell? Yes, and it smelled like the Happy Lounge, cloyingly sweet and sour at the same time with a tinge of Fabuloso cleaning liquid added to the mix. Michael knew the lounge well; he often had to find Uncle Robe in there and bring him back home. He hated this chore when he was younger but when he was a teenager, he would stay there a while with Robe who would slip him an occasional beer. He started drinking with his uncle and never stopped until he stopped, years later. By then Robe was very ill with unchecked diabetes, had his left leg amputated to the knee, and he was in a nursing home in Albuquerque. The Happy Lounge was a distant memory.

The Stillman's often had maids who attempted to clean the house. More than cleaners they were caregivers to Adoración. The list of their names was long: Any number of Marías, several Julias, Clorinda, Dorinda, Melinda, Delia, Mela, Any, Cany, Genoveva—the worst of the lot, the woman who stole Lety's wedding ring—Dolores, and so on. He remembered them all, but especially a few of them who were young or attractive. When Clem left home it was a good thing. He got married early and so he was out of the way. They never did get along. Michael got his room, which was the first time he had a room to himself. And he got his pick of the maids. Most of them were old or tired out or ugly, but there were a few who liked him and who he liked. His favorite was named Emma. She was from Juárez like most of the women who came to work for his family. Emma was in high school and very bright. She was introduced to the family by her aunt who used to work for them. Her Tía Mercedes was getting married and moving to California with her Anglo husband, Buster Creighton. Emma was off for the summer and came to work for the Stillman's. Small, delicate, and very lovely, she was also very shy. They barely spoke at first and then one day he stopped her to tell her he wanted to be friends. They never made love like he did with a few of the maids. They would meet in the family's bomb shelter and talk. Bob had constructed it several years before and it was stocked and ready to go. The eventuality never presented itself. Soon Lety began to use it as a storage room. It was built in the backyard of the Stillman house. It was the first bomb shelter in the neighborhood and one of the first in the city. It was a great expense to build it at that time in the 1960s, but Bob knew he wanted to protect his family in all ways. Who built bomb shelters then? Good grief, no one except cockeyed worrywarts out of touch with reality like Bobby Stillman. Lety wanted to know what he was thinking. A bomb shelter. Why? They didn't need a bomb shelter! They needed a new stove and to fix the roof or redo the outdated bathroom, but no! Bobby had to build a bomb shelter!

Michael's Spanish was pretty good. He didn't have an accent but sometimes words failed him. Emma's English was very good, so it didn't matter. She was planning on graduating from school and then going on to get a medical degree in Mexico City. She would move in with an aunt who lived there. Emma let him hold her hand and kiss her but that was it. He fell in love with her but there was nothing to do. He was still in school, she was still in school, and the summer passed.

Michael remembered those times in the bomb shelter when he lay on the long couch, stretched out, thinking. The Stillman's were people who lay around a lot. They were most comfortable slouched on a bed or sitting on one of their long beige couches and talking to each other and the relatives who would come over. And regularly, they sat around and talked about their extended family, the Stillman's and the Casados, and their antics. Most of the time they talked about the Casados. They were farmers who lived in the valley and were an unsophisticated bunch. The Casados were easy to ridicule and imitate. Ha ha. It was a funny family. Robe would sit on one of the long couches next to his daughter, Raquel, and he would imitate his brother Manuel, the one who was a janitor, or he would talk about Manuel's wife who left him for a friend, some mojado from Chihuahua. He did imitations of people, and he did voices. He sang sometimes too and most of all he made people laugh. Ha ha. They would all sit on the long couches and the time would pass as time passes. No one ever thought how fast it would pass. Lety would die of whatever she died of no one quite knowing what it was. Mostly, she starved to death because she couldn't eat. She lost all appetite for food, for living. Robe was in that nursing home up North, and no one ever went to see him. He who loved people and to be around his family was finally left alone. There were other siblings, but they were poor or crazy and lived on the Mexican side of town with all the other Mexicans. The Stillman's lived in the newer part of town, what was once cotton fields. They owned the fields that led from their house to the highway. And one by one, they sold a plot of land when they needed the money. Until finally, all the land was gone. The cotton fields ruined the earth, but few people realized that when they bought their land. They were happy to live on a street named Encantada in the town of Encantada in the state named The Land of Enchantment.

It was a small street in the newer, expanding part of town. A desirable place. Close to downtown. Close to the university. Close to the stores. Close to the post office. Close to the schools. Close to the hospital. It was a perfect place to raise a family.

Adelaida was the longest lasting maid. She worked for the Stillman's first, taking care of Adoración for several years. Most of the maids didn't last that long. A week, a month, a few months. There was a constant rotation of women of all ages. Once they found out what their job was and what they were expected to do, they quickly left.

Adelaida was an older woman who had a family in Chihuahua. Once a month she would go back home to visit them. The rest of the time she lived with the Stillman's. It was hard to say where she slept. Where did any of the maid's sleep? When you entered the Stillman house, they were always dressed, up long before anyone, with no sign of their lives anywhere.

In many ways, all the domestic workers were invisible women. They did their chores if they were not interrupted by crying children, the never-ending demands of the mistress of the house, or fielding the undesired advances of several sons, their uncles, and a neighbor down the street. If they were young, they would be addressed more respectfully, treated better, and almost made to feel human. If they were older, tired out, unattractive, too thin, too fat, too whatever, their life was hard from day one.

Adelaida was the only maid, and this is what the Stillman called all the women who served them, who became more than a slave. And yet, she still was a slave. But she was a slave with a name. A slave who was remembered. She was not ever family or really loved. She was a needed appendage like a thumb, but that didn't mean anyone cared for her. She was dour-faced, sad-eyed, long-in-the tooth, and like an older horse, she would have never had much of a chance working for anyone but this broken-down and dysfunctional family. And yet, it was a family.

Adelaida's responsibility was Adoración, that was her real work. And at this she excelled. She loved the old woman in all her mercurial ways and treated her like she should be treated, with respect and care. The same could not be said for the old and justifiably bitter lady whose charge she was. Adelaida, to her, was just another sirvienta, a servant who was there to tend to her needs. She felt nothing for the woman who got her up in the morning, gave her a gentle sponge bath, changed her clothes, sang to her throughout her duties, fed her with care and then took her into the living room in her wheelchair which was positioned right behind the large recliner that faced the front door.

It was a good vantage position and became the fortress Adoración needed to keep her removed from the world and yet close to whatever action that would unfold.

Adoración held her post in the middle of every turbulent day in the Stillman house, she was there when there were sorrows and joys, and she was there when the house came to life and then shut down for the night. She watched everything and said little. Her voice had frozen from lack of use and now she only made little sounds. An occasional word would come out and it usually had to do with her beloved son, Robe, who was never to be found. He would appear occasionally and those were always the best times for Adorácion when she basked in the light of her dearest son's life. She would sit in her wheelchair in the living room behind the recliner and peer over the edge to look at her adored son, the one who was her favorite. And why was that so? He was born prematurely, a weak child with blond hair and beautiful eyes. She named him after her father, Roberto, but there the resemblance was to end. Robe was a baby who cried all the time, he was often sick, he had long bouts of moodiness or sadness or whatever it was that made him fussy and anxious. He always wanted the breast. He was needy. His legs were weak, and he didn't walk until he was three years old. She had to carry him around everywhere and it fell to her to take care of him, often neglecting the others. She had prayed for his life as he was being born on that terrible long night during which she thought she would lose him and now, too many years later, she was still praying for him. He was a lost and hopeless child. He was her special boy. He was her one and only, her favorite—her consentido.

Robe stared at his mother's face in the mirror. No, it wasn't his mother's face, it was *his* face.

He had also seen his mother in the reflection in the sliding door at his sister Lety's house. No, it was not Adoración he saw, it was *his* own reflection in his wheelchair. He had come to visit one last time. And then he would go back to that place where he lived.

Look, there's Mama, he said to one of his nieces. He couldn't remember her name. She nodded and walked away.

No one told him it wasn't his mother. She'd been dead for many years now. It's best not to scare anyone.

If you look at yourself in the mirror and see your mother or your father, that's fine. Never be frightened. Remember you carry them inside of you. They are a part of you and after a while, some faces blend, some bodies adhere, and people mistake you for the ghosts that live out there in the other world and who once walked on earth.

Eres la misma they will say to you. But you know you aren't your mother. Te pareces a tu papá. You look like your father. But you know he was much different, and you don't look like him at all—and yet—there is that part of her or him in you. The parts you sometimes want to hide away or forget. The ugly, critical, bitter parts. You remember too often the sad parts and their tears. But do you remember their joys? You never knew their joys so how could you remember? You remember the difficult days, the ups and downs, and the struggles, but do you remember the other times? No. You just remember the pain. It was there, always present.

Sometimes you will visit your mother in your dreams, or you will feel the presence of your father. You will hear someone cough the way he coughed and remember your mother used to say she could recognize your father's cough in a crowded room full of people or at the back of a church during a crowded mass. The sounds of the dead still live among us, and in a street full of wind and dust and story, the voices sometimes rise and want to be heard. But to really hear you need to listen carefully. The wind is full of too many voices, too many stories, and to sort through them is the gift few are given.

It is a blessing.

It is a curse.

And always, there is the question.

Sisters, brothers, why have you left me with your stories?

The smell of red chile permeated the air. The harvest was over and now was the time for processing. The plant near the house was working overtime to process the chile pods that were the industry of the valley. The deep rich and hearty smell of chile made Michael happy. He loved so much about his hometown. He loved the food, nothing better than a red enchilada or a green, nothing better than the upcoming holiday season with his cultural traditions and its sense of connectiveness. It was the time when he felt the closest to people.

And yet, Christmas was nothing special to the Stillman's. In his large family, they drew lots and gave a gift to only one person. If that person was a sibling, they rarely got you any gifts that were worth much. What can children afford to buy other children? And what can the parents of too many children afford to buy even one of those children?

Michael remembered all those Christmases. Especially when he was younger and then later in high school.

The Christmas trees were always scraggly and misshapen. Lety was most likely to buy it on Christmas Eve when the prices were reduced. They would drive around town looking for a tree lot that was still open and she would try to bargain with the owner for a cheap one. The trees were decorated at the last minute with very old and shabby ornaments and silver icicles that were thrown randomly and clumped together as they were last year's decorations. The pitiful little gifts were assembled from where they had been hiding—in closets, under the bed, in drawers and made their way to the tree. The small, discolored tree apron was placed around the tree and the gifts lay there. Bob called out the numbers and one by one the gifts were distributed. Some years certain numbers got no gifts, that's the way it was. Who could afford gifts anyway? Presents were for families who had more than the Stillman's, for families that knew abundance.

Michael dreaded Christmas and the paltry offering his family made to each other. What he did like was the food at the neighbor's house on Christmas Eve. A businessman, Dan Roberts, was the wealthiest man in the neighborhood. He would host an open house on Christmas Eve at his large home for the neighborhood each year. There were large pots of posole, tamales, and wondrous desserts. This was where Michael first tasted divinity, the whipped egg confection that he loved. The Roberts children were friends and to be in their home with their family was a pleasure. They were a family that seemed so happy, so complete. Their tree was always tall and covered a large corner of the living room. It might be flocked as was popular in those days and often it was painted blue or pink. It was wonderful to sit in the Roberts living room with their blinking tree and know that all was well, at least, for them.

The smell of red chile filled the night with a dark longing. He was from this place and not. He loved this place and not. He wanted to leave this place, but he did not. He wanted to go away and never come back but he knew if ever he did leave, he would always come back.

On those walks late at night he began to become a friend to the many cats that lived in the neighborhood. And soon, he began to feed them. He had several feeding stations, one in an abandoned house in the middle of the street. The owners had moved away to a nicer, richer part of town and abandoned their home. He saw a skunk emerging from the darkness, its large and full tail sticking straight up. He was feeding the skunk as well as the cats and more than one racoon and it made him happy. Why not? The animals deserved to eat as well as any of the other animals.

When he went out on his walks, he carried a bag of food and water. His mother didn't like his feeding the neighborhood critters, but he circumvented her protests by hiding the bags in the storage shed. That was until the rats found the food and decimated several bags of cat food. Lety never found out, but it was necessary to move the cat food to the bomb shelter. No one went down there anymore except his father. What he did in there he had no idea. Maybe he just wanted to get away from everyone or maybe he took a nap. The bags were hidden in a corner under a tarp. Late at night Michael would do his rounds. He felt needed and he was.

Nowadays time always lay heavy on him. He preferred doing nothing, just lying about on a couch, resting in bed, or maybe listening to music. Music soothed him. He liked to listen to jazz. It took him far away and allowed his mind to rest in a place without words. Isn't that what music is supposed to do? Talk to you without words?

Linda remembered Michael in those days when they were teenagers. He was older, good-looking but goofy. He didn't know how to behave around people, especially women. She was attracted to him, but he was older and yes, odd. He always had a girlfriend, but they were a strange bunch. Some older, some hardly his type, some of them refined and maybe a friend of the family, later some of them blowsy and over-made up, and once, a woman with enormous nalgas. He showed up with her at a wedding and his "date" was wearing a diaphanous skirt that barely hid her enormous buttocks. She had on a see-through top as well. What was he thinking? He had the oddest sort of woman by his side. She imagined that they imagined that he cared for them, but he cared for none of them. He was incapable of loving. In the same way, she was incapable of loving anyone. Maybe they could work something out. Can two people who can't love anyone else find friendship and then maybe love each other? They were both alcoholics. They would understand that part of themselves. She was also involved in drugs once and was a member of Narcotics Anonymous, NA. She attended fewer of those meetings than she did of AA.

It was hell. All of it was hell.

She put on her makeup. She, still was good-looking, still young, still had a life ahead of her. Linda looked again in the mirror. Her left eye had started twitching. She was beginning to feel the chill again. When it came over her, she had to get in the car and drive. Sometimes she drove around town for hours. She would drive out to the countryside and stop the car and just sit there. Sometimes she slept in the car out there in the middle of nowhere. Sometimes she just sat smoking. Eventually she would find her way back home. First to her parent's home and then to her apartment. She was back home for good. She would never leave again. Not this time. She was here to stay. How long that would be, she wasn't sure. There was no way to get out of this alive.

How could things have turned out this way? What happened to her? What happened to the children on this street? What was wrong with their families? What happened to their fathers, to their mothers? Were all the children lost like she and Michael were?

It was nearly time to go out. She would go to the Sheraton and see what was happening. She wondered if that new band, the Brochures, was still there playing. Or maybe she would end up at the Happy House. It wasn't so happy, but she knew everyone there. It was the oldest bar in town, and it was known for its rough atmosphere, but it was the place all the drunks ended up at the end of the night. You would see everyone you knew there, all the old guys and their young dates, people like Michael with his latest girlfriend, his married brother Clem with his secretary who was his lover, the Bank President, that old stick of shit with a young woman who looked bored, the fathers who should be at home, the sad pathetic men and women who should all have been long asleep in their beds, all of them ordering last call as they tied another one on, chalked another one down. God Bless Them. God Bless Them.

All of them with their last words in their mouths. All of them with memories that swirled and sliced the air and made them sick remembering, all of them crying in their drinks, or laughing too loudly, with raised voices and the ugly, demented laugher of the lost, demons surrounding them in the pits of hell.

She often wondered what her last words would be. What would Michael's last words be?

They made a pact. Whoever died first would try to find the other in the swirling undertow of dreams. They would look for each on that road that went up and down and suddenly ended. They would find each other in that shuttered claustrophobic house with apparently no exit and help the other escape to air, to sunlight, to the stars. They would crawl out of the subterranean underbelly world that bound them to their terrors, and they would be there for each other, the way no one had been there for them, a hand stretched out, to help them cross that bridge, that crumbling staircase, the stairs going up and the building crumbling down around them. That hand would be there with its sure grasp. Fingers entwined, they would help each other climb up or down as was the case, to land on their feet, upright in the light of day.

She was cursed. As he was cursed. They were two of a kind. Maybe they could love each other. They could try.

Don't think that the street didn't have its mañas—its ways, its habits, its strengths, and its weaknesses. It seemed to be a street like any other street, it wasn't. For no street is alike. Each has its special qualities, its liabilities, its gifts.

Encantada Street was in a flood zone. In the past, the Río Grande ran through the area and flooded its banks during those years of rain. The course of the river was changed by the dam up North. Also, the years of drought brought change to the river and its path. Years of cotton altered the area and now it was hard to grow things for that mighty crop had leached and altered the land.

When it flooded, and it did occasionally, the street was dangerous and wild. The water might rise to a man's knees. Once all the families woke up to nearly waist-high water, flooded yards, water-logged garages and even a wooden beam floating down the street like it was headed somewhere.

The water rimmed all the houses with mud and there was an infestation of weeds that took years to overcome. It was a shock to imagine what the ancestors faced without protection and the ability to get away.

As a result of the last flood, the city decided to work on flood control. They put in huge pipes that diverted the water and it took years to finish the project. The workers didn't get it right the first time, so they had to go in again and do it all over, probably adding on another year. If you wanted to get to your house in the middle of the block or anywhere on the street, you had to walk in. This meant you had to carry groceries in your arms and park at the end of the street. The middle of the street was a gaping hole. When it rained it was horrible and of course, this set the work back months. There were those days when no work was done and this, too, dragged on and on.

There were a few years of terrible cold and snow. Feral animals were at risk and so were humans. It was hard to get warm that year. Most of the houses still had floor furnaces and few had central air and heating. Fireplaces were going full tilt. The neighborhood suffered with the cold and again with the heat. There were years of a hundred-degree temperatures for weeks. The heat could kill a man or a woman or a child and it did. You were advised not to water at certain times, not to work outside at certain times and to avoid the sun. If you ever had the misfortune to get sunstroke, you were marked for life. It was an insidious and debilitating and constant reminder that you had stayed out in the sun too long. That weakness remained with you always. You never mowed your lawn in the summertime unless it was very early or very late. God forbid you should have to climb on the roof or do anything major in the yard. And yet, the young and stupid girls still tanned in the middle of the day. Women's skin was permanently altered by the sun. The brown age spots began with the sun of those early and foolish days.

Anyone who lived on Encantada street always remembered it and the characters who lived in the houses. There was the neighbor who had an illegal Chihuahua business, keeping too many dogs in his backyard. Once they got loose and he was seen rounding them up in his pickup truck. One Fourth of July he set fire to a trailer full of his trash, blaming the fire on an errant firecracker that had exploded near his trash heap. He was not mentally stable—who was on the street—and lived with a much younger wife who was truly unstable. He came from a family that was known to have mental problems. His brother had once robbed a bank and left his driver's license on the counter.

Some houses had long living inhabitants, others not. Some houses had people that came and went and the wear and tear on the house showed. It wasn't a poor neighborhood, but it wasn't a rich neighborhood either. The people could be called middle class. They all had day jobs if they worked, and most did. There were a few stay-at-home wives, but most people worked outside the house.

For a while, it was a street full of young people, with their screeches, their high-pitched voices, and their pranks. Later they became teenagers and raced down the street in their parents' cars. Then, years went by, and mostly older people inhabited the houses. Strangers started coming in and renting. Fewer older families remained. The houses became shabbier, and the street grew smaller. Most houses had two or three cars that parked in what used to be a yard and often dirty mops would be draped near the front door. The yards became unkempt and messy, full of discarded furniture, toys, and appliances. It wasn't a new street anymore, but a tired old woman of a street with too many failures.

The houses were run-down with crumbling walls and battered wooden garages with slats of wood hanging over the side. The entryways were dirty with old carpet remnants and the neighbors began to lose their sense of pride in the street. Many of them were renters who didn't care and those people who did own their house were older, on Social Security and struggling to pay their bills.

The street has its stories: the night evacuation for a broken gas pipe. Everyone was asked to leave their home in the middle of the night. A few slept through the evacuation and were surprised to find out the next day they had been in peril.

Who chose to live on that street? A few old families. Most long gone. Some had moved away, never to return. Many were deceased. The relatives of the old families had new lives elsewhere, they didn't want to live on the street anymore, didn't want to remember their childhood growing up and their too-fast growing old. Many people had died in the houses on the street. They could be counted. Their deaths strong memories.

The street has its history, and still it was a relatively quiet and gentle street. There was something good about the street and those who stayed remembered the good. Those who stayed had enough good to remember. And those who had the bad lived miserably. The unhappiest died young and some of the older people died badly as well. One could chronicle the lives and tell the stories but somehow no one would believe them all.

It was a small street. It held its myth, its legends, and its dreams. Many of the stories were sacred and beautiful. Children were born in the homes and came of age and grew old inside the houses where they were born. Others came to the houses and never knew the sacredness of life that existed in its walls. To some the street was truly a home, to others it was a living hell. To some the street was a peaceful and quiet place, to others it was darkness personified. There was loss and lack and suffering behind the houses and there was joy and passion and release. There was singing and dancing and too much prayer. Untold never-ending rosaries at all times of the day. Feverish ambulance calls and the sound of women crying alone. So much was held in the houses and so much was withheld.

In the summer, the city truck came by to spray for encephalitis. All the children on the street ran out to become part of that cloud. It wasn't until much later that they all realized that what they had been running through was toxic. No one told them not to play in the street when they were spraying venom to kill the mosquitoes. Who knew then the many poisons that surrounded them and which they waded through and inhaled. Pollutants surrounded them and they had no idea. They were just children, and no one was there to tell them otherwise.

These were the children who ran through the street in the summertime with wet bathing suits. They had just emerged from a nearby swimming pool. Their hair was dripping wet and matted down. They wore cheap plastic thongs and had dripping towels thrown over their shoulders. They were a little cold but not too much. When they came inside to their homes, they ran to the bathroom to peel off their still wet suits. Their young skin was mottled, whitish and slippery like the skin of an eel. It was summertime and they were children. They were happy. They would never grow up and if they did it would take a while. They weren't in a hurry to learn how it was like to be an adult. They didn't have to pay taxes. They didn't have bills. They lived at home. Their parents took care of them. They had food, shelter. They lacked nothing or at least not now, not at this moment. They shed their bathing suits like a second skin and shivered with the knowledge that they were loved. They put on dry clothes, came into the living room and realized at that moment their great hunger. They scooped the watermelon from the middle without worrying about it and they satisfied their thirst.

Little children they were. Unaware.

It was only when they went to sleep at night that they became afraid. Something was waiting for them in the darkness. They peered out the darkened windows and imagined they saw someone standing out there in the street. They could feel things moving around in the room. Sometimes there was a spirit in the closet. They heard the music, far away then near. They heard the voices without bodies. Sleep came hard and late. And when they did sleep, they were still afraid. They were surrounded by evil.

Yet, there was something comforting about the street. It was small. That was a very good thing. It was like living in a small city. It was a community of people who all knew each other and tried to help each other out. Well, not everyone was a good Samaritan, but some were friends. The women knew each other better than the men and they liked each other. The men were openly critical of the other men and found them to be fools. Or at least that was what Mundo thought as he looked out the large picture window which his maid, Analuisa, had just cleaned earlier in the afternoon. He didn't really know her name but for the record, her name was Analuisa and she was a new helper. Vicky had recently hired her. She'd taken out an ad in the newspaper to advertise for a helper on the weekends. Her main helper, Diana, was getting older and didn't want to work weekends.

It was tough taking out ads because you never knew what sort of people would present themselves. She had to tell the men who applied that the job was already filled. Her father would never tolerate a man taking him to the bathroom, pulling down his pants, and then wiping him. Nor would he accept a man changing his diapers when needed. He was as homophobic as they came. Everyone was a joto to him and sadly, he was also a racist. There was no hiring certain people. And this included young and attractive women. Vicky even had to limit his television watching as he became too excited when he saw any women with little clothing or in provocative scenes. Not to mention people of color in programming. The time came when she sadly admitted to herself that her father, Edmundo Fuentes, was not a nice person. She always knew her father was reckless, irresponsible, a womanizer, undependable and abusive to most people and had been all his life. She now had to tolerate his intolerance and do the best she could to shield others from his ugliness. The effort sometimes wore her down. And she often found herself apologizing for his behavior. How humiliating it was to be connected to the crotchety and sometimes disgusting old man who was her father. And still, she loved him. And she knew he loved her. She was his daughter and there was that hard and fast bond, and it had to do with the fact that she really did care for him. Despite all his faults, he was her father. He had loved her mother Erme, and she had loved him. Vicky knew that there was something in him that was good or once had been good. What had happened to him? What had turned his goodness, his hope, and his talent into failure? Where had he gotten lost and taken that street that led to perdition? What kind of an afterlife would await a man like him who had harmed so many?

She looked over at him, eating his diabetic cookie and low-fat frozen yoghurt and she felt such an immense and overwhelming pity for him. And in that moment, she loved him and felt so sorry for the grief that had stolen his soul and made him incapable of loving. He was lost to the drink, and he never came back from that drowning. He could have been such a good man; he was so talented and so funny and so warm and so charming when he was with people. And he was that way with her as well.

When they went for a ride in the country he was like a happy little boy, so expectant and so glad to be out of the house. Coming back home was always hard. If she kept him out too late, he would get disoriented and grouchy. She hated leaving him in his house and going back to her own which was down the street, but she had to. He took so much from her and sometimes gave so little. And then other times he gave her the blessing of his true spirit, and this made it all worthwhile. She loved her viejito so much. Had she told him today? Daddy, I love you. And she knew he loved her back. She was the daughter that was there for him until the end.

Mundo looked out the window. It was still light. He could see down the street. The maid, whatever her name, was getting his supper ready. Victoria had just dropped him off and he was sad to see her go home. They'd gone for a ride out in the country, down in the valley. She'd also driven him to his old neighborhood as she always did. She showed him his old house where he lived with his parents and his brothers and sisters. That street never changed much. Poor, dusty, too many Mexicans. That was the world he left behind when he moved away. And now here he was, back again. Erme was dead these many years and he honestly missed her. He couldn't articulate to anyone what he felt inside. Erme knew who he was, the good parts, the bad parts, and he missed knowing someone who knew him when he was almost happy. With her he had had hope. They had their little girl, Victoria, and they were almost happy. They never talked about that child she lost. Clarita. It was too painful. She tried. He'd tried. He really tried. But it couldn't be helped.

It was that time of the day. Joe was sitting in his car reading the newspaper. Mundo didn't know how he could read it comfortably, what with the size of the pages inside that tiny little bug of his. He understood why Joe had to get away from Senaida. He would have as well. He remembered Sen when she was young. She was vivacious and loved to dance. She liked a good party and that's what she and Joe had in common in the beginning. Now you would never find them together or even in the same room. That's what Vicky told him. They were strangers to each other even though they lived in the same house.

He and Erme had been like that at the end of their marriage, although Erme was so much nicer and kinder, and yes, better looking. Although in her youth, Sen had been attractive. Now she had a shrill voice and always seemed to be yelling down the street to someone about something. He could hear her from his chair in the living room facing the street. She yelled at her kids, she yelled at Joe, and she yelled at the dogs and the cats, and sometimes she just yelled at the wind. He heard her talking to herself sometimes and it was unpleasant. If she wanted to yell at anyone she should go inside her house and yell in there. And she probably did. She was fed up with Joe and he was fed up with her. Thank God he and Erme had at least been civil with each other. Well, for the most part.

What Erme did was cry. And this was worse than yelling. He never liked women who cried. And all his life he had been surrounded by women who cried. It was intolerable. Tears made him sick. Crying women made him very sick.

Dammit, there stood Senaida outside Joe's car yelling at him. Didn't she have any decency? Good God, what was she yelling about now? It was around suppertime, but he knew that they ate apart and in separate rooms. Anyway, that's what Vicky told him. Not that he cared. He didn't care about them. It was just the drama of it. Them out there on the street, him in his car and her outside yelling about some goddamn thing for all the world to hear.

Where was Victoria? Why wasn't she here?

Victoria! Victoria! He called out. Victoria!

What is it, Mr. Fuentes, the new woman said. Do you need something?

Dammit you scared me. Who are you? Where's Victoria?

She went home. She was just here, and she went home.

Where's Victoria?

You live here and she lives down the street. This is your house.

This isn't my house. I don't have a house.

This is your house. You live here and she lives down the street.

Where's Victoria?

Do you want a cookie, Mr. Fuentes?

Dammit, who the hell are you?

My name is Analuisa. I'm here to help you.

Who are you?

Analuisa Peralta. I'm the new person.

Where's Victoria?

She's gone home.

Take me home.

This is your house, Mr. Fuentes. You live here.

This isn't my house! I've never had a house. What are you talking about? Let me talk to Victoria. Dammit, they're out there in the street.

Who are you talking about?

She's yelling at him, and he won't open the car door.

Can't you see them? They're out there again. She won't leave him alone. I would lock myself in the car as well if I were him.

Do you want me to close the curtains?

Goddamn it. You can only take it for so long. Then you have to move away. Lock the doors. I understand.

How about a glass of milk with a cookie?

Dammit, who are you?

Christmas on the street was magical when Victoria was younger. Erme went all out to decorate the house with angel hair, which nowadays is hard to find since it is spun glass and possibly toxic. But in those days, who knew? Erme filled every bowl with glass bulbs that were missing their ends and were unable to be hung. It didn't matter as they looked just fine in the bowls, the ends tucked back. Wreaths of red and white hung from each room entry and there was mistletoe as well. The tree was always a nice tree, not like the Stillman's but not as large or pretty as the Roberts the next street over. The house was always nicely decorated with festive ornaments and her many nacimientos, the creches that she so loved. Erme was a spiritual person unlike Mundo and Christmas was her season. The record player would be going full time playing the likes of Perry Como or Mario Lanza singing Christmas carols. The Little Drummer Boy often played in the background and Christmas music from around the world. The air was charged and expectant. Victoria knew her mother had many gifts for her and that she would go to bed on Christmas Eve with a new wardrobe. She and her mother would attend Midnight Mass and when they got home, they would open presents. Often Mundo was there, having returned for the holidays. Erme would cook his favorite foods, carne adobada, cows' tongue, tacos, huevos con chorizo, calabacita, arroz, fideos, with sopaipillas or biscochos for dessert, and they would lounge about Christmas Day, only stepping out to visit relatives. That day was usually cold. You could see your breath and fortunately no one had to go far, maybe only down the street.

Those were idyllic days that Victoria missed.

The reality was this: her mother was dead. Long gone. Her father was now her charge. There was no way he was going to go away, not for a while, whether she liked it or not.

Michael was never a good student. He had decided to major in Architecture. He was a good draftsman but somehow the work didn't suit him. He left college in his sophomore year and moved to New York. He got a job there with a public relations firm. It suited him better but still he wasn't happy. He didn't know anyone, nor did he care to meet anyone. After six months he came back home. His father gave him a job at his realty office and that's where he stayed. He was a real estate agent now like his father was. Bob retired years ago and left the office to him. If ever there was a dead-end job it was this one. What was there to sell and to whom? He had no interest in the work and yet had done very well in business.

It was close to Christmas, and he was back at the Arid Club. They were having their Christmas party: a potluck dinner with lemonade and coffee. Linda Chapa was back in town. She once had a glamorous travel job in Europe. As a travel agent she visited many countries throughout the world. Life was exciting for her, or so she said. Why then was she back home?

Christmas. Christmas meant nothing to either of them. They left the party early and went back to his apartment to talk. She shared with him stories about growing up down the street. Stories she'd never told him before. Afterwards he told her about his life, his sorrows.

This is why they made love. He felt sorry for her. She felt sorry for him. They felt sorry for each other.

They weren't in love with each other. They did like each other, they understood each other, but each was too absorbed with themselves to ever feel real love.

Linda could never love him. He was divorced and never remarried. He never talked about Nancy. Linda had never been married and had many lovers, on every continent. Michael had many lovers as well, all hometown and homegrown. What could they possibly offer each other?

I have to go, Michael.

Stay.

I have to go.

Where? Where are you going? Back to your dad's house? Are you over there?

No, I rented an apartment. I'll never go back there. This time I'm staying; I'm staying for good. I'm applying for a job. Administrative secretary.

Good. That's good. No, I mean it. It's good!

This time I'm sticking around for more than a few months. I just can't leave; you know how it is. I love this place. I hate this place; I love this place. Let me get my things.

Stay. You can stay.

I'll see you back at the Club.

I'll be there.

The days were getting colder. Christmas came and went. It was the coldest winter Linda remembered living in this town. She brought out her heavy coat and wore long underwear most of the time. It was an unusually bitter winter. She was chilled all the time. She, who had lived in cold countries and knew what cold really was, felt the coldest she'd ever felt. Her hands and feet were always frozen. She slept with socks on and a cap. The thermostat was always set high. If anyone would come over, they would have found it too hot. Not that anyone ever came over. Well, those few she allowed in. Sometimes Michael sometimes someone who she fancied. This was seldom and mostly she kept working. Working. And she read a great deal. History. Novels. Biographies. She liked autobiographies and reading about the lives of people and how they bared their souls on the page. It didn't take much. Could she ever write the book she wanted? The book she had been waiting all her life to write. She wasn't sure. She wanted to write that book, but damn, it was hard to write a letter, much less a book. She did keep a journal, but her entries were boring and sporadic and disparaging and sometimes just dull. Her life was that way. She was on the rollercoaster of her mid-thirties without a clear future in sight.

She remembered the day she felt most alive, most attractive, most vital. She was traveling in some southern state, somewhere in the U.S., on assignment from her travel agency. She had taken the day off and was reading by the swimming pool. No plans but to read and turn in early after a meal at the hotel. An older man approached her and invited her to dinner. No thank you, she said. He noticed she was reading Stendhal—The Red and The Black. It was an exciting and awful book at the same time. She wondered what he thought of her, a young attractive woman reading that book in the middle of his world. He told her he was a lawyer, something professional, not just anyone. Would she like to have dinner? Just dinner he said. But she knew he wanted more. He was intrigued. What woman would be reading Stendhal in the middle of the deep south so far away from where she came from?

No, I'm sorry she said.

She knew he was married. But that wasn't it.

She had the choice to say no. And she had.

She was so completely in her flesh that day. She was alive and well and so completely herself. She was alone in a world so very different from her own. But she knew who she was and not even Stendhal would deter her from saying no.

She kept reading. When she finally finished and went inside, she was very sunburned. Her perfect day?

Good God, that was her perfect day? A day alone just by herself at home with a bottle of booze. A long nap. An early dinner of whatever there was, a nightcap or two or three, a good book or a movie on the television and her little glass nearby. What else? She could feel the sleepiness coming on, the slight buzz of relaxation and it moved over her like a gentle little cloud. She was under the cloud's protection and felt sheltered there. The phone was off the hook. Who was there to call? What was there to say to anyone? She would take her glass into the bedroom and put it on her nightstand. It was right there, her little friend.

She took out her journal which was in a drawer on that same little nightstand. Another swig. Ay, yes. Now what to write in her little book? She wanted to leave some nugget of wisdom in her journal. There wasn't much to say tonight. She was leached out and tired. Last night had been another night. She'd cried and remembered things. She was full of mercy and forgiveness and felt sad for herself and for her father.

Good God there really wasn't much to say tonight. She put the pen aside and put the journal away. She had to sleep. She hadn't slept well in weeks. She had a terrible stomach ache for weeks in the pit of her stomach, more under her sternum. As if someone had punched her there in the pit of her body and rammed their fist up into her chest. She couldn't eat much and yet she ate as if nothing was wrong. She wondered if she should go to the doctor. And then one night she'd taken out her journal and began writing. That night the pain left her. Now it was more constant.

Does life work that way? You carry pain in the deepest core of your body cavity, and it rises as you confront the people who hurt you and who you hurt? They come up and get inside your head and start moving around until you tell them to leave you alone? Sometimes they do leave and sometimes they don't. And when they do you sleep and when they don't you get up and take out your pen and the notebook and you begin to write the story of the story.

You can barely keep your eyes open, and your body is tired, so very tired of staying awake when all you want to do is go to that bed and cover up and close your eyes and sleep. Sleep. Sleep.

This can't go on. The stomach pain comes back, and other pains and you wonder what it is that is holding you gripping you haunting you and it's almost too much to bear. And so, you take another little sip and yes, it feels so good. So good. Too good. To be under that little cloud, in the shade, resting.

The street had its stories, but they were never the stories that you expected to be told. Somehow things changed.

The fathers were never the stories.

The father's stories are not what matters now. The fathers need a rest. They want to rest, and we need to let them rest.

The father stories are old, tired-out, buried—like the father's. All the fathers are now gone, long gone, and the stories about them are a history that has ended.

The mother's stories are still to be told, and the mothers do have some powerful stories.

The children are what matter in this story.

The children are who they are because of the fathers and the mothers but it's more than that, it needs to be more than that. We are not our mothers. We are not our fathers. Their spirits reside in us, but we don't have to live their lives. They had their choices. They chose how to live their lives. They are gone now to an eternal place. And yet, still many of us live our lives choosing our father's anger or despair, living our mother's pain and distress, wondering why we are so cursed and why things have happened to us the way they have. When will we be free of our fathers, our mothers?

Many of us are still hooked to our fathers, our mothers.

Imagine your body with giant hooks coming out of the front. The hooks emanate from the front of the body and slice through the interior of your flesh. From a giant hook hangs your father. From a giant hook hangs your mother. From a giant hook hangs your brother, your sister. Your husband or wife. Your lover. The major hooks are those from our most immediate family. Some of the hooks are from those people we have allowed into our lives. Those people unnamed except in the darkness, late at night. Those people we loved desperately, without telling.

Imagine now unhooking.

Linda heard the woman's words, and she knew what she was saying, but somehow it was hard to do what she said. The woman stood behind her. She could feel her hands moving in the air. She was stroking her without touching her and her hands shifted to a downward motion, as if cutting through something.

Unhook. Unhook. Now imagine I am cutting through the light wave of that energy and just slicing it, slicing.

How do you feel?

Linda felt silly. And yet she understood what the woman was saying.

She was beginning to let go, to be unsliced or unhooked. Well, she thought she was anyway. She couldn't really tell. She did feel different, but she wasn't sure if she was unhooked yet.

I see a little spot there, some residue, leftover emotion, unresolved issues, misplaced feelings. Do you feel it?

Yes, she felt it all.

We can work overtime. I see some father energy there. Oh, and over here. . .who is that, your grandfather?

Linda never knew her grandfather. Neither of them.

The hooks were still hooked. Suspended, she was between worlds, the real, the imagined, the light, the dark, the inner, the outer. She floated in the air, the hooks in her back, as she looked down into the abyss. In the dark place she was afraid to look, the place of ultimate terror, she saw the endless world of her guilt. The corpse of her aborted child came up to greet her. It was the child she couldn't care for because she was too frightened to be a mother. It was a mistake, her mistake. And Michael's.

She left town again soon after they'd gotten together. She never told him she'd gotten pregnant. It was so surprising, so unexpected. They were only together that one time. He wasn't aware she was carrying his child. She could never tell him. She was guilty, yes. She had wanted it to live, but it wasn't possible. She had tried with all her might to keep it alive. But the child never survived.

She was incapable of being a mother. And that's what she saw when she looked down in the abyss of her greatest fear. She couldn't love her child the way she should have. The way her father couldn't love her. The way her mother might have loved her if she too, hadn't been afraid.

The hook was still there, embedded in her skin. She would never tell Michael. She was sure he never wanted children. They didn't love each other that way. They were only friends. Drinking buddies without booze. Neighbors for the longest time. Pals. Best friends. She knew him better than he knew himself. He knew her better than she knew herself. Blood brothers. Kin. Family without being family. Vecinos. They knew the same stories, lived on that same street, and went to each other's birthday parties. Ate the same white cream birthday cake and drank the same Hawaiian punch. Played tetherball. Swam in the same pool. Jumped in the street and kicked the small ball into the neighbor's backyard. Yelled at the same dogs to shut up. Shouted at the same cats to get off the street. Went to confession to the same Catholic priest at the same church. Father Roybal. A Spaniard who was an alcoholic and had more than one mistress. Knew and hated the same nuns. Loved the same third grade teacher, Mrs. Morales. Walked back the same way from elementary school. Went to the same junior high. Loved the same flavor of ice cream. Started drinking around the same age. Loved drinking. Loved fucking. Loved that people liked fucking them. Felt superior sometimes and realized it was really their feeling inferior not superior. Were actually shy. Really shy. Loved music. Loved singing when they were alone. Liked being alone. Loved people who left them alone. Liked anyone who they could be alone with and who didn't need to talk. Didn't like being in crowds. Never cared for cooking. Preferred eating out. Hated oppressors. Hated hypocrites. Hated cruelty to humans. Hated cruelty to animals. Loved silence. Loved the middle of the night when the world was asleep and seeing the sun come up in its brilliance. Loved going to bed early and waking up in the middle of the night or very early in the morning with plans, solutions, ideas, moments of great insight and creativity. They were creative people, both of them. They saw this in each other. They saw so many things in each other. Too many words unsaid.

In another world, in another galaxy, in another time they would have become a father, a mother, bringing into this world a child, perfect and complete.

Listen to me. Concentrate on the pain that you have there, in the middle of your stomach. Higher. There, under your rib cage. What is it?

It's as if someone had forced their fist into Linda's stomach, brought that fist up and jammed it into the middle of her body, hit her hard when she was least expecting. She didn't see it coming. The pain wouldn't go away. It had to go away.

I see a person standing in front of you with their hand like a weapon who rammed you with the power of their unspoken rage.

I see the traces of that old pain. It will eventually go away. Or maybe it won't. But you'll be different, and you'll understand it. We'll work on it. And soon, soon, you will be completely un-hooked. Do you feel better? Let me slice that invisible chord. That's your father. There now, it's better. I'm cutting that little edge of sorrow. That's your mother. Now turn around. Let me look at you. Your face is clearer. You look better. How do you feel?

The woman went on talking.

I feel your mother popping up again over here.

Well, yes, she would pop up. That was how she lived, here one minute, gone the rest. She was usually not found. In a house so small, where did she hide?

Do you feel the release? I see it, I see it!

Well. . .It was worth a try. It was all worth a try.

Hypnosis. Reiki. Diet. Psychoanalysis. Chocolate. Booze, Mota. Sex. More sex.

She'd tried them all.

Some worked for a while, some worked longer than others, some never worked. Some made her feel stupid; some made her feel superior. Some made her feel worse than she felt before. And one or another made her feel almost alright.

She never wanted to scream again into a pillow. She never again wanted to hit another punching bag. She never again wanted to face another person with her legs folded in front of her and tell them she was a little girl and that her inner child was in pain. She never wanted to utter the phrase inner child again. She never wanted to stand in front of a nun, a priest, a shaman, a guru, a teacher, a mentor, or her best friend. She never wanted to say the words completion, closure, forgiveness, or acceptance.

Completion. When?

Closure. What the hell?

Forgiveness. Maybe.

Acceptance. Never.

Adelaida had been shelling pecans all day long. Yesterday as well. How long can you shell pecans before your fingers bleed?

Her hands were wrapped in bloody bandages. No one seemed to notice or care. She was only the hired help. What did it matter if her hands were torn up and bloodied? It would have taken little to take the large costales of pecans down the road to the pecan farmers or the business whose job it was to shell pecans. No one had thought of that. It wasn't for lack of money. It was because no one thought of it.

She was a simple woman, and this was the work she did for a living. Her patrona, La Señora Stillman, had hired her out to her sister who had a large home and was always throwing parties. Adelaida still took care of Adoración in the beginning but now her full-time work was at Lety's sister's house. The sister, Maggie, was wealthy and had recently moved back to town from Back East. Her husband, Randy, ran a loan company back in New Jersey but he was retired now. Or at least he had planned to retire when he moved to Encantada, Maggie's hometown. First his brother-in-law, Bob, borrowed money. Then a friend of his came asking and before he knew it, he was lending money right and left. The high rates didn't seem to bother anyone at first, they were all so desperate and in need. He found out that people were willing to pay him to lend them money. It seemed foolish not to loan them money at a high rate. It all worked out eventually, didn't it? And if it didn't then he wasn't the one who suffered.

Randy didn't like Maggie's cleaning woman. She was an old woman who didn't speak English. And yet, somehow, they communicated on a very basic level. Usually, Maggie was there to intercept. He wasn't home much. He was either traveling back and forth to New Jersey to oversee a few business deals out there or he was on the golf course. When he was home the old woman was usually tucked away in the kitchen or in her room. She was efficient, he had to say that about her, old horse-faced boot that she was. Maggie had come to depend on Adelaida to clean the house and tend to all the details of the parties they gave, many for family members. Thanksgiving was in a few days and that's what Maggie and the old maid were getting ready for. He hadn't ever really called her by name. He wasn't really sure what her name was. Something with an A. Sometimes she was so quiet he forgot she was there. That was good. She kept out of his way, and he kept out of hers. That's one thing that was good. The other was that she was a hard worker. Usually, Mexicans were. People from Mexico that was. He didn't know about these half-assed people who said they were Mexican Americans or worse, Chicano, whatever that meant. He wasn't sure. He did know that Maggie was Mexican American. The good thing was that she wasn't stuck on it, never carried on about being Mexican this and that and feeling she was superior about her roots. He had married her because she was lovely and nice. There was something innocent and unspoiled about her. He met her when she was working in a nearby office. Once he proposed, she stopped working. Now she had a monthly budget to take care of the house, all its needs and the old woman who took care of her and him, of course. Not necessarily in that order.

You clean the bedroom? He asked the old woman.

She looked up at him with that aged and inscrutable look that could mean anything.

You clean-o?

¿Mande, Señor?

Room de sleep? Okay?

Sí, Señor. She mumbled and went back to shelling pecans.

Maggie loved pecans. She was known to put pecans in nearly every dish she prepared. She was a great cook and loved to entertain. Pecans went into the cornbread stuffing. They were to be found in the candied yams. The pecan pies and the Mexican wedding cookies were full of pecans. Pecans graced the long elegantly decorated table, each plate with its gold charger, each setting with its rolled napkin in its gold napkin ring. In the middle of the table was a large vase full of flowers with gold sprayed pomegranates and gold sprayed apples. Their decorations were always something to see. Loose nut plates lay around the rec room where everyone gathered to play pool, get a drink at the wet bar, or just lounge around on any number of large plush couches and chairs. A huge, big screen television was set to the sports station and the sound drowned out the voices of relatives who came to the golden trough to eat the rich family's food.

Adelaida continued shelling pecans. She sat in the walkway between the enormous and impeccably clean kitchen and the immense recreation room where all the action took place. She was about finished with the last costal of pecans and it was good. She had been working on the pecans for days. She had gone through three bags of around 45 pounds each. She was tired. But she said nothing. What could she say? She would be going home soon with the money earned and gifts for her grandchildren.

Since she'd left Lety's house things had changed dramatically. She now had her own room at the back of a large house. Maggie gave her many things: clothing, furniture, quality things she would never have gotten at Lety's. In many ways, things had improved. She wasn't taking care of her viejita anymore. She missed her. Better to not think about her or she might start crying. She had loved her viejita very much. She'd gotten attached to her and to be without her was hard.

Adelaida didn't miss all the children and their coming and going. Most of them were grown up but they kept coming back. And there was Lety who needed care herself. And there was the brother, Robe, who was a disaster. He slept late, was messy and always drunk. She learned how to take care of him when he came home after a night of drinking. She would bring him warm milk and put it by the couch where he slept. Later he moved from the family room to another back room where he had more privacy. When he was back there, he might sleep for a day or two. Lety would let him sleep off whatever cruda he had and then he would leave as if nothing happened. He was friendly enough when he was sober but Dios

Mío, he was an ugly drunk. All bluster and vomit and bad words. No, it was good she'd left that festering and smelly house for this one. Maggie's house was big, spacious, and luxurious. She didn't have to sleep in the storage room on a cot but had a very nice room of her own with her own things. She had come up in the world.

She didn't mind the hard work and the constant attention Maggie needed. Maggie was good to her, in her own way, and sometimes they talked about all sorts of things. She wasn't a mean patrona. She was little butterfly of a woman, flittering but never landing.

What Adelaida didn't like was him.

El Patrón.

It wasn't anything he did. Or said. Caray, she couldn't understand one single word he said. And yet, she did understand him. And he probably understood her. He was a big hulking man. And White, very White. How did he and Maggie ever get together? She was small and delicate and ladylike and he. . .well, he was big. Too big for her. He had a very big head and hers was very small.

But she wasn't paid to think about these things.

She had about a half hour to an hour to go with the rest of the pecans. That's if nobody bothered her. Most likely someone would come up and ask for a ladle or wonder where the wine glasses were, or they wanted ice or something like that. She was on call from the moment she got up until the time she went to bed.

She thought of Lorenza, her daughter in Juárez. She missed her grandchildren, Ricardo, Javier, and Paty. She would see them at Christmas. She had the week off. Maggie would drive her to El Paso and leave her by the bridge where she would take a taxi home. Or maybe she would take a bus to save money. She worked hard all month for them. Lorenza's husband had left her, and they needed help. And then there was her son, Ismael. He'd lost his job at the factory. He and his wife, Chela, were expecting another baby.

The pecans were Maggie's favorite—she loved her pecans, and this was the place to love them. They grew in the region and were known for them around the world. She didn't like them much. Her teeth weren't so good anymore and nuts were hard on her. She had a cracked tooth that hurt her sometimes and didn't want to aggravate it any further. When you get old you have to watch your teeth. There were so many things she couldn't eat now. She loved chicharrones but they messed with her stomach. She liked cheese but it gave her gas. Meat was too hard to digest, and it sat heavy in her insides. She ate little and tried to take care of herself as best she could. She didn't like most of the food Maggie taught her to make. It was rich, heavy, full of salt and coiled up inside her like an untamed animal. She fixed her little meals on the side and ate her avena and atole and drank her herbal teas. Better this way. When she went home to see her family, she brought back her té de manzanilla and her Estoma Curol, which she took faithfully to regulate her body. She needed to go home to get some more.

But first, she would finish with the pecans and ask if La Patrona needed anything. If not, she would slip off to her room and put her hands in warm water to rest them. Then she would wait a while and come back and clean up after the party. Then, only then, would she go to sleep. It had been a very long day.

The sunsets on Encantada Street were spectacular. The sky turned a glorious and indescribable rose color with a lustrous and luminescent blue infused in the middle. The sky was electric, filled with a wondrous light. It was such a pleasure for Vicky to walk down the street and know she lived in such a beautiful place. There was no place like her hometown, and she knew it. She had traveled very little and always rushed to get home. Why was that she often wondered? She'd had conversations with her neighbor, Linda, and asked her what it was that she loved about traveling. Linda had lived all over the world, mostly in Spain, and France, and other places in Latin America when she worked in the travel business. And yet, she always came back to their little hometown.

What was it about home? In her mind and heart Vicky was a small-town girl. Large cities scared her. She wasn't sure how to maneuver and the getting there and the getting back were leaps of faith. She prayed going and prayed coming back. She wasn't a religious person in the typical sense of the word—but she did believe in the great spirit that held the world in its hands. Call it male, call it female, the spirit was greater than the words that men or women used to articulate the Divine.

The sunsets on Encantada Street were moments of the Divine.

Today was a peaceful day. Yesterday not. But the good days outweighed the bad. Her father was resting now and that made her feel calm. She had to remember to breathe, to calm herself. He was an old man, not well. He was often angry and unpleasant, and he yelled. He was her charge and hers alone. It was a lonely place at times, no one to step forward to help in the way that would have really helped her. An occasional call from a relative would have been appreciated. Mundo's brothers and sisters were all older, some better off than others. No one offered to help monetarily. It would have meant so much to have that extra hundred dollars a month or a bag or two full of groceries. His relatives never thought of coming over with food or offering to help pay for his caretakers. And she never did ask them. Did it ever occur to her? No, not until now, years down the road. Her viejito's house was empty. Her viejito was buried in the old Mexican cemetery, close to downtown right next to his wife, Erme. That would have made Erme happy.

When her mother died Victoria bought three burial plots, one for herself, one for her father and an extra. The extra one, de pilón was there, on hold. Erme had left her a little money, how she never understood, as she worked hard all her life and never made much money. Her father, on the other hand, had a good job with the state and never saved a penny. Her father left her nothing at all but bills still pending at the collection agencies. She was grateful they were in collection. She paid off his bills $10 and $15 at a time. All the years of him living on Encantada street her father never had any money. His social security was little, as was his retirement. It was a constant struggle to pay his caretakers and his medical bills and to buy groceries, but somehow, they'd made it all those years.

Walking down the street facing west, she remembered the many times she'd walked east toward Mundo's house. He was always happy to see her. And he was always a little sad when she walked home. Walking west now she wished she could walk east and greet her father another time. Hi, Daddy, she would say. And he would be happy to see her because after all, she was his only daughter. She was the one who stood up for him, as his legal guardian and power of attorney. She helped him with his physical needs and saw to it that he got the best care they could afford and yes, suffered with him all those rides to the hospital in an ambulance. How many times she'd prayed for him. Too many times she asked the Divine Mother Father to spare him, heal him, take him gently into that darkness without fear. She didn't want him to choke to death, he who had the small throat, he who was apprehensive and afraid of death. She counseled him, fearful herself, and somehow grew stronger throughout those years of his illness and eventual passing.

The west was where her father lived. In the sky of all possibility and hope. His was a vagabond life, without much except Erme's love. He did redeem himself in Vicky's mind, for he suffered in ways she would have never foretold. A man who didn't need anyone, a man who lived alone and wanted the alone to be with his beloved drink, an occasional woman to fill his emptiness, he was to most a pitiful sort. He had lived a mess of a life. And yet, he did much good. Or so she heard from others. He could be very generous. She knew that. He had been generous to her in ways she would never have imagined.

Walking west down the street, around the corner and then back, she was thankful for so much. Her house was near her father's and that was good in those days of his need. She so often felt guilty leaving him in the custody of so many others. The hard thing to admit was that she couldn't live with him. He was too difficult and demanding. And there were his demons to think about. They often hovered round. She often had to pray for herself coming and going back and forth between his house and hers. She was often upset and angry leaving his house. She often cried on the way home or in her house, in her room and on her bed, thinking of him and wondering what she was going to do this month, the next. How was she going to pay the caretakers? Did they have enough money for groceries? When was his next doctor's appointment? The worries were so many. And she was so ill-equipped to be her father's caregiver.

Facing east, she remembered all the days of suffering. It could make her cry until the tears wouldn't flow anymore. But she was tired of the tears and the worry wasn't there anymore. Her father was past her worry. Those people she'd loved were past her worry. She'd done the best she could have done at the time. She was young during her father's illness, and she thanked God she could lift a wheelchair into her car and push him along and yes, lift it over a doorway and take him to the bathroom and help him into bed and change his diapers for that day came as well. It wasn't a problem. When are diapers a problem? We are all children shitting and carrying on. What's the difference? She wasn't squeamish and did things that needed to be done when they needed to be done.

Facing east, she remembered the anger, the sorrow, and the grief. She also remembered the laughter and the joy. She loved to shop for him and buy him things. He was easy to please and liked new clothing, a bright shirt, soft pajamas, a plush throw rug, comfortable tennis shoes. He liked to eat despite his throat problems and with care he ate everything and enjoyed it: pizza, oysters, hamburgers, enchiladas (not too hot and made with a Campbell's soup base), Sloppy Joe's, liver and onions, shrimp, the list went on and on. Victoria often ate lunch and dinner with her father. She sat in the dining room, and he ate alone in the living room, a tray table in front of him. He ate best when he wasn't disturbed. And yet he knew she was near, in the other room, and when he had finished eating, they would sit and talk and sometimes watch television. She would give him his life story, the pointers, and highlights of his life. She would tell him what time it was, what day of the week, and what was new in the world. As she gave him his life tapes, he listened to her. She was his daughter, and he did love her. He played the tapes back in his mind and he was content. She was happy as well. She loved him, irascible old man that he was, still handsome, with his tiny, wizened battered head from so many falls and cuts and bruises. He had been beaten several times before she found him bloody and battered on his couch. She never knew what had happened. He had a head injury, and it was hard to say what caused the dementia—the alcohol, the beating, or the wearing down of his life by all his illnesses. He was her charge. And she accepted it. Facing west, she felt the blessing of those years. Facing west, she understood now what she didn't understand then. Too many things. Too many things. Too many things. And out of all those many things, she took the one thing and made it hers: forgiveness.

The rattling of leaves against small rocks. The rocks bouncing on the street against twigs. The twigs swirling against the pavement. The spirits came up fast on him. Michael faced the directions to see where the wind was coming from. It was always good to know if the wind was at your back or coming toward you. The ever-gaining cold was moving in as night settled on the street. Knowing that the wind was headed west was good. Suddenly a giant gust of air skirted past him, and he felt the bodies of an army of creatures' swirl past him. The ancestors were out tonight. They wanted to dance in the night. It was a good night for them to leave the confines of their other worlds and to land on earth again. Close to those they still loved, close to the places they still yearned to visit, close to the earth they once walked, their twirling formless spiraling forward toward their present eternity of invisibility. And yet, they were seen for that one moment by that one person. He heard them throwing small stones in the night, heard them in the trees and in the shrieking of a cat and the cat's owner swearing and yelling at it. And he without thinking rushed forward to help that poor animal saying, "What's going on?" only to have his neighbor yell out, "Fuck you, it's none of your business."

And yet, it was his business. His business was talking to the spirits who had called out to him. The many who moved through the street not thinking anyone would see them, not realizing his ears were so attuned to the smallest most minute sound and the sounds behind and below those sounds. He heard them, heard their soft movements in the night street, playing like children do with rocks and dried sticks their chatter and jostling moving the clods of dirt as they kicked and played with the refuse on the street, the random paper that found its way to the sidewalk and the bits of fluff and cat hair and paper bags that looked like small wounded animals in the street, piles that lay and did not move but mounded and became testimony to the random displacement of nature objects that became something he would pick up later, something he would clean and throw away, something that reminded him of the spirits who played with each other in the night and passed the houses where they once lived.

The spirits peered inside to see their families, what was left of their families, writing letters, reading books, watching television, cooking a late or early dinner, resting on the bed, taking a needed shit and then brushing their teeth, washing their faces clean of makeup or sweat, putting on their nightclothes or taking off all their clothes, getting under the sheets, laying down and falling asleep or not, doing a slow or fast recapitulation of their long or short day, remembering what transpired, planning or not planning for a tomorrow that might or might not come, making plans and lists in their minds, remembering what they needed to get at the grocery store. Counting the objects they needed, one, two, three. Figuring out how much money was in the bank that day, what needed to be paid and on what day. Wondering how they were going to pay this bill and then the next and figuring out how they were going to be able to pay the mortgage or the dentist or the taxes and wondering how they would feel tomorrow after weeks of suffering with a bad stomach, sore knees, a pain on the left side. Liver? Kidneys? Lungs? That little pain in the back that spread to the middle of the back. The twinge in the solar plexus. The tooth that was delicate and needed to be worked on. The pain in the pit of the stomach or the groin. Wondering how the rolls of fat came on and how it was that the rolls begat their own powder and beaded skin that flaked to the touch. Their flesh was once young and fresh and yes, it was soft. Now it was soft but not fresh. The skin hung in places and their faces began to wrinkle. That's how it was.

The spirits saw all this as they moved down the street, peering in the windows, looking through the rusty grates that were once painted bright blue. The spirits stopped on the porches of their old houses and saw that the steps were broken, and that the sidewalk was cracked. They saw the lawns dried out and the empty lots full of tumbleweeds, an old tire that had been there for months, garbage piled in the corners, the weeds overgrown and now browned. The spirits saw it all and they said nothing. They just observed the state of things. That was their penance. To just look. To just see. To just wonder. Not to assist or declare or reclaim. They were only able to move from that place they now called home to this earthly place briefly, their former life gone, but still remembered. How humans agonized! How humans suffered! How humans cried!

The spirits moved quickly through the street with the western wind that carried them back to their homes in the sky in the clouds in that world beyond where they lived. They saw everything without judgement. They were patient and they would wait for their time. They would wait for the moment when their loved one looked up, felt their presence, and knew for certain they had passed. The penny was there on the pavement. A bird's feather was waiting on the sidewalk. The glass bead was in their path. A flock of crows flew overheard. One crow called out in the night. Another crow danced in the parking lot in front of their passing car. They called out with the voices of dogs, cats, birds. The birds cawed and said their names and flew into the corners of a grocery store, momentarily trapped, hopefully only for a short while, inside that giant place where people came and went, where rats came out at night to eat the dog and cat food and the edge of the cheeses, and the life inside knew the life outside.

The spirits danced in the street not knowing or not if anyone person heard them but yes, someone did. Michael stopped to listen. The rattling of small rocks was a giant clatter of sound in the night, and he stopped to listen to the world turning, turning. He felt a sudden rush of wind move past him and he knew that the street was full of people coming to visit. They were headed back to where they used to live to see again with their spirit eyes those who they had loved, still love. They wanted to see how they were doing. And why should they care, after all? They had moved on and didn't need to worry anymore about anyone or anything. And yet, they did. More out of curiosity than dread they looked around corners and moved invisibly through walls, because after all they were spirits and had no bodies. And although they had no bodies some of them became trapped in those houses and those rooms and were stuck—for a short or a long time—they didn't know exactly how lengthy it would be—maybe centuries or maybe just an instant but to be a spirit and be trapped in the house of memory even an instant was a torture.

Spirits need freedom and the wind to carry them from place to place and back again to that refuge they called home. It would be hard to explain to someone what place was to a spirit. There are no words for that description of place to a human or an animal who knows a fixed reality. Imagine vast space and an ever-expanding sky. Imagine flight and the freedom of movement without effort. Imagine colors unseen and a darkness within the darkness. Now imagine a light within the light. A sound within the sound. Imagine hearing the heartbeat of a leaf and the cry of a tree. Imagine.

Michael walked down the familiar street. How could it be so small and so full of story? He turned around and felt a sense of peace. It was the west wind that he felt coming at him. He knew it was the ancestors who had moved past him and were headed home again. There it was again, the rattling of small stones, the crunching of something underfoot, the gnashing teeth, the growl, the clenching, the smacking, the humming and the beating of wings, the small imperceptible movement of something out there talking to him. Asking him to stop. To listen. And he did. There were no words. Only the wind again at his back carrying him home.

The rattling of a discarded soft drink can. The crinkling of a random paper bag thrown from a moving car. The screech of brakes at the end of the street. The police car siren in the distance. The country western music from a nearby radio. The hum of the houses as they settled in for the night. Feral animals in their designated sleeping places, the restless and young still moving, still eating, still licking, and cleaning themselves. The animals sought shelter from the growing-colder nights. Settling in, resting against each other for warmth, the older animals knew the winter was coming but they weren't afraid like the humans inside their warm houses. Each took every moment in stride. Accepted what was. Then lay down to rest. To sleep. To dream. For all creatures do dream. They dream of those other worlds, those other places. The places that can't be named.

Those places the spirits go after they've scurried down the street. That familiar well-loved street. The street the humans thought they knew so well.

It was time again. Thanksgiving. The people she wished would have invited her to the late lunch or the early dinner, hadn't. Someone she didn't know very well did. The woman worked with her at the university. She had a large family and knew that Linda was alone. It was a kind invitation, but she declined. She didn't want to sit around all day waiting for food she knew would be good and listening to the family stories of a family that wasn't hers. Nothing more boring.

Her family stories were just as boring but at least she knew the stories and knew the people and could add something in response if she felt like it.

She would say to her brother: grow up and start treating your wife with respect. You're neglecting your children and although they're grown, they will remember you were never there. To her mother she'd say, what happened to you? Why did you stay in the marriage so long? I know you barely spoke English, didn't drive, and never managed a bank account, but Mamá, so many times I asked you to come and live with me. We would have made a place for ourselves. It would have made me so happy to help you out. But you were too timid, too lost. And then you got sick. Mamá. What happened?

Papá. For you I have few words. I can't say what I want. You talked but you never listened. You spoke so little to us said so little. You made us lose our voices. And when you were gone and we could speak, nothing came out of our mouths.

Here I am a thirty-year-old woman, and I can't speak to anyone in our family. I can only talk about myself to strangers.

My name is Linda and I'm an alcoholic.

Thanksgiving was always hard. This was the time of the year when Papá was home and when he came into my room all the time.

Mamá was in their room with her headaches and her woman pains and the bleeding that wouldn't stop. It made her go to bed and stay there for days. We didn't know she had cancer and that a hysterectomy might have helped. But she was too shy and wouldn't see the doctor. No man could touch her and there were no women doctors that anyone knew about for miles. All the doctors were older Gringos and even though they were older Papá wouldn't let them look at his woman. He was an old fashioned Mexicano, and he was jealous of all men, all men who dared to look at his Marielena who still was a beauty. He wanted her in the house doing her work, doing the things she should be doing as a mother and a wife. Why should he allow a pinche Gringo the chance to look at her and see her the way he saw her? And yet, she was very shy. She undressed in the closet and dressed in there as well. She went to bed covered up and woke up covered up. He never saw her fully naked and standing in front of him, not even on their wedding night. She was so young then that he waited for her that night and a week had gone by, and she was sleeping on the floor in the front room of that little apartment. She had a little mat, and she would bring it out and then bundle it up in the morning. At first, he was willing to accept this. She was, after all, still a child and knew nothing of the world. But the night came when he ordered her to bed. She came to him, unwilling, and would stay that way all her life.

She didn't love him, he knew that. And if truth be told, he didn't love her. He liked certain things about her, her youth, her beauty, and yes, she was soft and compliant. She never felt too much for him. And he knew it. There was no passion between them. She would never know what love could be between a man and a woman. She never grew up, that was the problem. She was always a little girl and thought and felt things like a child.

What hope was there for them?

Marielena had their children, but she was disconnected from them all. She would go to her room and stay there alone most of the time. At night she would undress and get under the covers. She would feign sleep and soon he would leave her side and find his way to his daughter's room. In the beginning, he just lay next down next to her. That first time he fell asleep next to her. Marielena found him there in their child's bed and said nothing. If only she had stopped him, corrected him, confronted him. But she didn't. She never would. When he left her bed to go to his child's room nothing was ever said. It became so easy to say nothing and to feel nothing. They were people who rarely spoke to each other. They were afraid to speak to each other.

Mi'ija. It's Papá.

Linda was sleepy. Papá had come into her room. Was he coming to wish her goodnight?

It's late Lindita. Papá has to rest. Can I lay down a minute and talk to you?

He did lay down, but he didn't talk. He said nothing but just lay there for a long time. She finally fell asleep.

The next night he was back.

And the next.

And soon Papá was sleeping with her all the time.

Mamá's sick. She needs to rest and be alone.

And she believed him.

And then one night he asked if he could touch her knee.

Thanksgiving was a day that came and went. Just like Christmas. This year Linda wanted to spend the day alone. Her brother had invited her over to eat with his family and she would try to get over there. Manuel was a good man and she loved him. But there was so much noise and so much movement, she wasn't sure she wanted to be there. It was ten years since her mother had died. Five since her father moved away with the woman who later became his wife. She heard that he had died over there in California. The funeral took place with those people over there. She didn't know then, wanted to have nothing to do with them. She didn't know he'd died until months later when one of her father's cousins called to tell her.

It was Thanksgiving. She would call Michael Stillman. Still single. Still a loner. Still going to AA meetings. Still a friend. She never told him she was once pregnant. Why? She wasn't strong enough for herself. How could she be strong for that little baby? It wasn't possible.

She was attending AA as well, just not at the Arid Club. It was distracting. She knew everyone there. She knew all their stories, all their jokes, all their bullshit roundabout lies to themselves and knew when they were back drinking, near to falling back and just pulling in again to sobriety. She knew their ups and downs and turnarounds and more than that, they knew hers. She had a new sponsor now. A woman, Eileen. She was a tough Black woman and she saw through all of Linda's crap. It was a relief and a blessing. She was doing well on the other side of town away from her old cronies and her neighborhood. She'd been able to walk to the Arid Club, but it was much too close to home. Getting in the car and driving out made all the difference. The journey was necessary, needed, and allowed her time to think again and to resolve again and to jump in again into that cold water of sobriety that she so desired.

She had started going to Narcotics Anonymous—NA meetings and finally admitted to herself that she needed to address her sexuality. She'd slept with too many men and a few women. She never loved any one of them. They provided temporary comfort. Relief.

She was still an attractive woman. Very attractive.

It was time to go. She didn't want to be late to Manuel's. She might swing by Michael's and see if he was there. He still lived in the neighborhood. Even though he was well off, he still rented dinky little apartments and never had much. He lived simply. She never did. Money came and mostly went. Her apartment was cluttered, full of clothing, furniture, things. It was always messy and yes, she was a hoarder. She collected anything that could be collected.

Manuel had tried to help her out when the landlord came after her to clean up. She was always in the process of downsizing. It never seemed to work. And now she had started gaining weight. She had to buy new clothes because the old ones didn't fit anymore. But what if she lost weight, well she would have to keep the old clothes, wouldn't she?

She'd changed from a size four to an eight and then to a ten. Most women would be so happy to be a ten but to Linda it was upsetting. She started purging and that's when the other thing came on. She couldn't eat and wondered if she suffered from anorexia. Or was it just stress? She made an appointment to see her old family doctor. He was an old man now and would soon retire. Dr. Klein knew her family and took care of her when she got sick as a young teenager. That's when the Dr. found out what was happening. She remembered how he took her into his office and asked her what was happening.

She lied.

Tell me, Linda. You can trust me.

She lied.

He knew it.

And she knew he knew it.

They were a family who spoke little. Their mouths were sealed. When they spoke, dust rose up and filled their throats.

Tell me. Tell me, Linda. I want to help you.

She couldn't speak but mouthed the words: Sweetheart, just let me touch your knees.

The Boys and Girls Club truck was parked in front of Senaida's house for a long time. It was impossible to imagine that all those boxes with all that stuff came out of the house. Linda could see two men move boxes into the truck for what seemed hours.

The garage sale had gone on for a long time as well, if you counted the magnitude of what laid out in front of the house in boxes and crates, what rested on tables, what was lined up in bookshelves and what was also spread on tablecloths in the yard. It was the worst of all garage sales because it was junky and messy and spilled all over the yard onto the vacant lot next door. Linda had gone over there to see what was going on and see what Sen had pulled from the house to sell. It was a heap of crap in her opinion. There were many boxes of books, paperbacks, and hard covers, some alright, some downright battered with a few decent classics in the mix. There was a set of the Little Women books with about half the titles that might could have been a good buy if you needed the titles that were there. A children's tea set in a wicker basket for three dollars was a very good purchase if you wanted it. Linda felt tempted. But what would she do with a children's toy tea set? Women's clothing was heaped in no order on a six-foot table. A pair of souvenir Indonesian miniature dancers stood in the middle of it all surveying the melee.

No sooner than Joe died Senaida had decided to sell the house. After all, it was her house to do what she wished. Too many bad memories. So much had gone on in that house. She'd had enough.

She wanted to get as far away as she could from Encantada Street. It hadn't been enchanted at all. More of a nightmare.

Joe was gone and it was an ugly passage after all. Oh, who knows, maybe it was peaceful. Sen would never know. She didn't know he was sick to begin with. Each maintained separate bedrooms in distinct wings of the house and she never wandered over to his side. She did notice he was very quiet that last week. He didn't come out at the end. It was several days before she noticed the smell. It was a strong and pungent odor like something rotten had died, an animal under the house perhaps. A raccoon? A skunk? Maybe one of the many neighborhood cats had gone under her house to keep warm near the floor furnaces as the days got colder.

Well, it wasn't an animal. It was Joe. She had to call her son over to have a look and see what was happening over on that other side. Ronnie found Joe dead in bed.

No wonder he hadn't come out. Well, imagine that. He was dead.

The house was in their joint names as was everything else. She had secured the papers years ago when they were first married and still were what people would consider a family. Now all the property and his social security and pension would go to her. Paltry sums that they were. And still, it was hers, wasn't it? She deserved the house, the car, the social security, and every bit of the insurance money he had gotten for himself over the years. He was an insurance nut and in the long run, that was what he was worth. The insurance. The house was old, run-down, just like the car and the furniture. The possessions, well, forget it.

As soon as the insurance money came Sen would buy herself a new car and a condo on the other side of town near the mountains.

There wasn't much of a funeral. Too expensive. She had him cremated and that was that. The ashes. Don't ask. She would never tell. His children were the few people at the funeral celebration—yes, it was a celebration, and she had a party at the house. Potluck. Some neighbors came over, Linda, a few of the deceased's kin. Not her relatives, they were related in name only, but they brought over food and some beer. Fine. Good the deceased wasn't around to drink it all.

And now everything Joe owned was near the curb where the Boys and Girls Club truck was loading it up. The clothing and shoes and what personal effects he had would go to the Gospel Rescue Mission for the homeless. What personal effects did the man have? Hardly anything. No personal photos of himself as a little boy, not a copy of his birth certificate, no Boy Scout badges or high school or college diplomas. Nothing. His shoes were old, his shirts were old, his coats were old. Everything he had was battered and used-up.

Sen hadn't wanted to see him lying in bed dead. Ronnie called 911 and the police arrived soon after. She refused to enter the room and identify him. Who else would be in that room anyway, she thought. His son is standing there, he looked just like him. Ronnie was handsome and tall and yes, dammit, he looked like Joe. She was cursed. Her son looked like his father and every time she saw him, she would think of Joe. No, she wouldn't. She and Ronnie didn't see each other that often and he was in the service. Good. He would be sent far away. As for her girls. Well, she saw them now and again. None of them looked like Joe. Her daughter Alice looked like her mother's side of the family. Good. Veronica didn't look like anyone in the family. Good. And as for Gloria, well she looked like Sen. Good. Someone to pass on the genes to. The good genes.

The ambulance came and took Joe away. She signed some papers, and he was gone. Just like that. She hired someone to clear out the room and clean it, some maid of her neighbors, an old woman named Adelaida. She wasn't looking for work full time, she was just a loaner.

Sen called a realtor. Too expensive. She decided she would sell the house herself. Good. It was better that way. She wouldn't have to pay a commission. Good.

When the Girls and Boys truck left there was still a pile of boxes on the side of the house. They stayed there a week or two. She'd have to call someone else to take them away. Her nephew or Ronnie if she could find him.

Linda felt she should offer to help Sen, but she couldn't bring herself to utter the words. Sen was full of hate and rage and would spend her time bashing Joe until she was red in the face. Let the man rest, Linda thought. He's gone, you have the house. He won't bother you anymore.

And then Sen moved out. Well, almost. The house was full of her plants. They had taken over the living room and were still there long afterward. She would come over and water them when she remembered. The living room was like a hot house. She tried to give some plants to Linda. No thank you! Most of them were ancient spider plants and Aloe veras that had outgrown their pots. The jungle of plants had overrun and taken over the front room.

Linda followed the progress of events. She had to. Sen was her neighbor and was once a friend. She remembered going over to see Sen now and again, just to visit. They would sit in the kitchen and talk. Linda was still a young woman and Sen was older, married. Somehow, they became friends. That's when Sen gave her or rather lent her a copy of her favorite book—*The Sun is My Undoing*. Was there ever a movie made from the book? Linda didn't think so. And yet, in her mind she had played the story back and forth. It was the first adult novel she ever read. It made an impact on her. It was part of her sexual awakening. When she read it, she realized the extent of her abuse.

Sitting in Sen's tiny little kitchen at her tiny vintage table she knew she could talk to her neighbor and friend about anything. That time lasted a few years and Linda grew older and the walk between her house and Sen's grew longer. Maybe Sen was her first adult friend. Linda loved her laughter when she did laugh, full of derision and deprecation. She railed against life, all men, especially one man. And yet, Linda knew she was a good woman because she was kind to her. She couldn't imagine anyone else letting a skinny little teenage neighbor come over to talk and maybe have a glass of juice or something to eat. Alice, Sen's daughter, was Linda's age, but she and Alice were never really friends. She liked Alice but Alice didn't really care for her. She couldn't say why. That's the way it was with so many people she could have been friends with. For some reason people didn't like her. Some were envious, maybe jealous of her beauty, yes, she was pretty, and she knew it. But more importantly, she was talented and intelligent, well-read, and well-traveled. What was it people didn't like about her? Men always liked her, and she had to watch them and their motives, but few women dared call her friend. She was good friend material except few noticed. She was loyal and supportive and kind. Few people saw what she was really like. They just saw the sexy, flashy, colorful exterior that she presented to the world.

Sen was her friend. She couldn't take her plants. She was sad to see Sen move to her condo. After she left the street Sen traveled a great deal with friends and loved to go to Las Vegas. She never came back to the street.

And then one day the plants were gone. Hanging in a corner of the living room where one giant elder of a spider plant had taken over was a white wedding dress. It hung from the ceiling. There was no one living in the house. It was empty, devoid of furniture, not even one plant left.

The wedding dress hung there for months.

Linda went over to see what was going on. The back door was cracked open. Perhaps someone was living there, a street person or someone from the nearby homeless shelter. She was a spiritual person, after all. On this street you had to be. Prayers were what kept the street from falling into an abyss of brimstone and ash, the nearby ever-present fires of hell.

Linda would have to ask Sen about the dress when she saw her. She wondered if she would ever see her again. Sen was gone. And the dress was all that remained.

The street knew the stories. Out of the many stories came the one story that filled the air. It could have been one person or another, it could have been one family or another. Who was to know what story was to be told and at what time?

It was surprising that out of all the stories this story should float up and fill the sky. But it was time. The story needed to be told. She wanted it to be told. It had to be told. Maybe her story would help someone. A young girl. A mother. Who knew who the story would help?

It was time to begin.

Linda Chapa's story filled the sky at sunset. It was a story full of fury and blood. It was a story rich and deep and sad. But it was also a story of bravery and strength and goodness. She was a good woman and she had done her best.

What is the history of a person's life?

Birth.

Childhood.

Teenage years.

College Years.

Professional Years.

What is the true history of a woman's life?

At age six her father began to abuse her.

At age ten her neighbor abused her. He was the husband of her next-door neighbor.

At age twelve she was fully developed and one of her teachers abused her.

At age fifteen she started drinking.

At age sixteen she had sex with one of her neighbors at his house when his mother wasn't home.

At age seventeen she was an alcoholic.

At age eighteen she started college.

At age twenty-one she graduated with a Fine Arts Degree. She was drinking heavily but secretly at this time.

At age twenty-one she got an internship in New York and left home for the first time. She wanted to be a journalist.

At age twenty-three she was still living in New York. Her boyfriend at the time was a drug dealer. It was he who introduced her to cocaine. She had smoked mota in college, but she hadn't gotten into anything else.

At age twenty-four she tried heroin for the first time. She didn't like it.

At age twenty-four she again tried heroin and did like it. But she preferred alcohol. This was a turning point in her life as well. Her boyfriend died of an overdose.

She cleaned up her life and moved into an apartment with a roommate.

At age twenty-five she was working for an advertising agency and making good money. She would go back home once or twice a year to see her family. No, not her family. Her mother. Her father tried to make love to her, but she rebuffed him.

At age twenty-eight she became a travel agent. For six years she traveled around the world and learned various languages: Italian, French, German. She already knew Spanish.

By age thirty she was using alcohol and drugs full time.

By age thirty-eight she was living back home. And she was broke. She decided to get a master's degree in counseling.

By age forty she had a master's in counseling and was working at the university as an Administrative Assistant to a Dean.

At age forty-six she decided to go back to school to major in English. English? Yes, English. She loved to read and wanted to become a teacher.

At age forty-eight she began to have blackouts. This was when she stopped drinking and rejoined AA.

At age fifty she was sober for two years but then she started having serious liver problems. She never told anyone, but she was very ill. Who was there to tell? She knew she was not well but there was nothing to do, not really. She knew she wouldn't live to be an old woman.

Her mother was dead. Her father was dead. She was back home living in the old house which she was renting from her brother who had bought the house when her father died.

The street had its stories.

Who knew the real stories of all the people on the street? Everyone's life was private or should be. What did one person know about another? Did they care?

Who knew Mundo Fuentes? His wife Erme? Victoria, their daughter?

Who cared about Rafa Chapa or Marialena?

Who bothered about Bob Stillman, his long-suffering wife, Lety? Who really cared about Michael Stillman? Michael didn't care about himself or anyone else. So, why would anyone care about him?

Joe Blanco didn't like people. Not really. He liked to drink but mostly alone. Senaida loved to be around people. But not her husband, Joe.

Who was there to care about anyone?

The story of the children is tragic. They were all sacrificed on the altar of their parents' insecurity and illness. For the parents were all sick people. To a fault. They didn't know what it was to be a parent, to love a child without caring for themselves first. It was obvious the parents cared more about themselves than their children. Heartless to say this, but then again, it's the wind who whispers this. It's the dust and the cold and the night that allows us to look inside the houses and to tell the stories of those who lived their lives on the street. The night tells us the stories of the people in the houses that brought forth the broken children. The children who later abused, drank, lied, bullied, killed their dreams willingly and the dreams of others. It is also the street where the children brought forth other children who abused, lied, drank, bullied, and killed the dreams of their children.

Tell the wind to stop. Tell it to rest. Tell it to go to sleep. We're tired and want to rest. It's late again and the stories come spilling out like blood from a wound. I am afraid and don't want to tell you what happens next. You can imagine. No, you can't. I never expected things to turn out the way they did. Yes, maybe I did. The children were not well. They came from people who were not well. Appearances were just that: appearances. Everything seemed fine. They were educated people for the most part, they weren't stupid, the children graduated from high school, some went to Catholic School, others to public school, but they were good kids, came from good families. They were mostly Mexican Americans. And you know how those families are: religious, tight-knit, private. They were told to keep things in the family. And they did. They were not flamboyant people. They had a sense of decorum. They kept up an image. Tried to. Let me count the ways. They were good people. Decent people. Let me count the ways. They weren't loud. They never made scenes. The police were never called. You couldn't hear anyone yell. No one ever screamed. Their dogs stayed in the yards.

They didn't roam. The cats were wild but that was expected. Sometimes the cats lived with one or two or three families. That was fine. Each household had different names for the same cat. In this household he was Fluffy, in another Grey Boy, in another Roger. Everyone took care of that cat. Their yards were neat for the most part. Codes never bothered anyone for overgrown weeds or stray animals. Everything appeared to be normal. Everyone seemed to be happy. It was a nice neighborhood with clean yards and well-kept houses. No one was rich but everyone seemed comfortable. There was no poverty here. Not in this neighborhood. No Black people ever lived on that street. No Asian people ever lived on that street. Only Anglos and their Mexican American wives lived on the street or Mexican Americans. Most of the children didn't speak Spanish because their parents were American. They wanted their children to grow up with English as a first language. The parents knew that to be a Mexican was a hard life, especially in this town. It was close to the border, but it wasn't México. México was another world. Another set of problems. Other frustrations. Other misplaced dreams. This was America. And everything was possible.

Maybe not for the parents, their lives were a jumble of confusions, a madness of love misplaced, a longing for things not attainable. Life lay heavy with the parents. They were from the old school, learned the hard way of their parents who lived a life of poverty, misery, and dread. Hoping their children would find hope in the U.S. of A.

Listen now. There had to be hope for the children. There had to be hope. If not then, what was the purpose of it all?

You can do it. You can. The children all heard these words. Maybe not spoken aloud. They knew they had to succeed, their lives had to become more and greater than their parents' lives. Who were their parents? Who knew their stories? Their aspirations, their daydreams, their fantasies?

Who had time to look into their parents' faces and ask them: Mamá, tell me your story. Papá, who were your people? Who were they and where did they come from? Who was your mother? What was your father like? No, we didn't have time. Each of us was absorbed with our own separate grief. And just how and what did you imagine your life would become?

The wind blew through the street. It wasn't late yet, but the nights were chilly. Poor feral animals out there in the cold.

The houses were warmer inside. The floor furnaces never heated the house fully but if you stood on top of the floor furnace the iciness settled down. You would stand there, legs spread slightly as the heat moved up your legs and soon you would be hot and ready to move away. That's how it was in the houses. At that time. No one had central cooling or heat. The houses all had a fireplace, but few families made a fire. It was too much trouble. And there was the wood to gather and the fire to tend to and somehow it all seemed so much of a bother. The people were too busy anyway. And no one was home long enough to make or tend a fire. Everyone wanted to get away. To go far away. To never come back. That's how it was then. On that street. In that town. At that time.

Walking home from downtown. The nightly walk down the street. A half-moon. There was the smell of smoke in the air. The street seemed fogged, backlit by something hovering out there, nearby but still far enough away. Somehow the faraway always ended up in the middle of the street, filling it with something intangible, undefinable. The night was expectant, anything could happen. And hopefully, it wouldn't. If you lived on Encantada Street, you always lived on the edge of dread. An ambulance might be rounding the corner, coming for the older neighbor, any one of them in those days. One by one the elders got sick and passed away. Priests came and went, and once the bishop showed up to give the last rites, but Mundo Fuentes started screaming and drove him away. It was a good sign. He wasn't ready to die. Not quite yet. One by one they died off. Nothing was ever expected. They were there and suddenly they were gone. Joe was dead, had been dead for days and no one noticed, not even his wife who lived in the same house. De repente, Marielena Chapa got sick, first her heart and then something with her lungs. She took to her bed and died. Erme had trouble with her right leg and slowly whatever it was creeped up to her hip and then moved to the left leg and then she couldn't walk. The next week she was in a coma and never recovered. Lety Stillman's case was the strangest. She was literally skin and bones and no one knew what ailed her. The doctors couldn't figure it out. She was hallowing out from the inside out. Mr. Fuentes, Mundo to no one really, woke up one morning and he couldn't talk. The next day he couldn't swallow. His daughter Vicky called 911 and an ambulance came to take him away. He was terrified and the susto never left him after that. He remembered that his mother, Paquita, was terrified of doctors and hospitals and when her diabetes got so bad and she was facing the amputation of a leg, she preferred to just stop eating. No one could talk her into living. She preferred to die with all her limbs intact. Mundo died in the middle of the night calling out Erme's name.

Most of the priests prayed in English, a few in Spanish. When Lety was near the end and what an end it was, there were two little Spanish priests who came and hovered over her like fruit flies. She found comfort in the fact they prayed in Spanish. The last months of her life she only spoke Spanish. For some reason, all the English in her was gone, left her just like that. Lety was perfectly fluent in Spanish but rarely used it with her family, with Bobby or with her neighbors. She did speak it with her mother. Adoración. It was hard to communicate with her youngest children who spoke mostly English. The older ones like Michael and Clem understood part of what she was saying. She mumbled and was sometimes unintelligible. It was as if her tongue had dried up and she couldn't use it to form words. Her skin was parched as if she'd been on a remote desert island, perhaps looking for shelter. She had a brown cast on her face, and she looked desiccated. And she was. The two little Spanish priests prayed hard and fast in their heavy Spanish athentos and with more amens that had ever been heard in that house. Lety wasn't that religious but near the end she hung onto her rosary and found it comforting. It made Bobby peaceful to see her asleep with the rosary in her hands. Her passing was excruciating to him. The children didn't come around much except for Michael who tended to his mother as best he could. She fought him and they had to bring in a woman to help. Lety thought it was Adelaida and called the woman by her former maid's name. Yes, it was comforting. One of the diminutive Spaniards had terrible B.O.—his body odor filled the room and as much as people wanted to be near Lety, it was hard. Few people wanted to be near and maybe it was good the odiferous little man was there. He kept people at bay as he recited the rosary in Spanish in her dark bedroom.

Lety was surprised to see her mother standing at the foot of the bed. Yes, she was standing! How could that be? Adoración hadn't walked in thirty years! And there she was standing on two good legs as if nothing was wrong. She looked concerned. Lety wanted to say something to her so she wouldn't worry. But nothing came out of her mouth. It was dried up, full of dust. And when she tried to open it, a small brown moth came out. She remembered Adelaida talking about the ancestors and how sometimes they appeared as insects, most particularly moths or bees. Bees? Bees! The old woman was insane or at least addled. She had very strange thoughts and wasn't to be trusted with her impressions of the world.

When Adoracíon died, Adelaida's peculiarities came forward and she became the laughingstock at the church. When the casket was wheeled out by the chunky director of Salgado Mortuary, she began a loud wail that didn't cease until what seemed like an hour later. It may only have been ten or twenty minutes, who knew? The only one to carry on and cry like that ever in the history of St. Teresa's Church was the old Mexican maid, Adelaida Hurtado. No one knew why. What had possessed her? Why was she carrying on like that so shamelessly? She had been the old lady's fulltime caretaker for a long time, but that didn't mean she had to embarrass herself that way. What was she crying so loudly? Is that how they do it in México someone said. It's a Mexican thing someone else commented. Those people don't know how to behave.

The crying was relentless and interminable. The Stillman children were mortified. Bobby didn't know what to do and tried to talk to the old woman but when he neared her, she let out a whoop and a holler that scared everyone. It was horrifying and ugly really the way she carried on. Finally, finally, there was an abatement, and this diminishment of noise was the sign for the priest to come out and hastily conclude the ceremony. The priest turned out to be the little stinky one who was wearing a white chasuble that was rimmed in sweat that could be seen from the front rows of the church. Oh yeah, really? Well, maybe not, but it could be imagined. In addition to his sweaty armpits, he had a foul breath that was the result of several festering and rotten teeth. Oh yeah? Well, it was possible, and it could have been the case. Something had to explain his condition.

Adelaida's hysteria abated, and she sat in the pew whimpering and rocking side to side. She had loved her viejita and it was just too much. Too much.

Thank God the casket was closed.

The family stood up after the final blessing, walked out quickly and swore to never again invite Adelaida to another funeral.

It was just too surprising to acknowledge that Adelaida would carry on the way she did. What had overcome her? No one had ever seen anything like that in the church or in the history of funerals in town, and there were many. Her cries came from a backward culture and from people who had no sense of decorum or culture. Didn't she know you don't cry out in the middle of a church service like that? The little sacerdote was taken aback and began to sweat more profusely. The two altar boys moved away and had to be coaxed to come closer to assist with the incense as the priest went round the coffin and blessed it several times.

It was quite a funeral, and it was remembered for a long time. People spoke about Adoración—her funeral and the cacophony of noise that rose and greeted her spirit as she moved to a better world.

¡Ay! The air was full of smoke and haze and fog tonight. The dogs barked at every turn and if someone walked through the street, they went wild. A nearby cat fight took place behind the house. What was going on? Just what the hell was going on?

Memories of standing outside near the street flooded Linda.

She was wearing a new dress she had gotten for her birthday. One of the boys she went to school with drove by in a car. She was sure he saw her. She saw him. He was one of the cute boys in her class. There weren't many and he was maybe the cutest. She was sure he saw her standing out there in her wonderful new dress. She hadn't planned on being out there when he drove by it just happened. Maybe he noticed her, how she looked. Maybe he thought she looked pretty standing out there in the sunshine. Maybe.

But when she saw him in class there was no recognition. He never acknowledged seeing her or driving by. As a matter of fact, he never looked at her, never looked in her eyes. Maybe it was that time, maybe it was their age. Few boys looked you in the eyes in those days. They never saw you. And if you looked them in the eyes, they berated you for looking at them. Why are you looking at me? They never saw how young you were, how pretty. She remembered that dress. It was her favorite. Navy blue and green, a summer dress, sleeveless and cool. When she went to bed that night, she put the dress next to her on her twin bed. She wanted it to stay there and be there when she woke up. But in the middle of the night her father came in and pushed the dress to the side. It fell on the floor. The night was very long and hot. It was summertime. When would school start, she wondered. When?

He was a fellow student at the university, but he was older. He looked like he was a fully grown man, and she was just a freshman. Everyone looked up to him because he was one of the top students.

He was very mature or so he seemed to her. His name was Reldie. He never looked at her and he had a girlfriend already. Reldie's girlfriend worked part-time in the history department office. They were both mature, older. She was his girl, and he was always coming into the office to flirt with her. Linda thought that Reldie never noticed her. And he didn't. She was very surprised that after school one day he asked her to go to the movies.

The movies?

When?

Today.

Today.

Right now.

Right now?

Hey, you want to go or not?

She thought they were going to a sit-down movie theatre and that he would buy her popcorn, candy, and a drink.

But instead, Reldie took her to the drive in.

The drive in.

He never bought her popcorn, candy, or a drink.

Even now, years later, she couldn't remember what the movie was. She didn't remember seeing any movie. As soon as they got there, he unzipped his pants and pulled out his penis.

She'd never seen such a large penis. Not that she had seen many. She'd never seen one that size.

Reldie unzipped his pants, took out his penis and guided her hand over to his crotch.

He never kissed her, held her hand, or even said much.

She laid her cold hand on his penis and yanked and yanked and yanked. It was an ordeal. She didn't know what she was doing, and she felt his frustration. He mumbled directions to her, but she was lost.

He had brought her here to use her. That was all. As soon as he was satisfied, he zipped up his pants and started the engine. They drove back to the university in silence. He left her in front of their department. He never mentioned anything to her, and she never mentioned this episode to anyone. It was a bad dream. It couldn't have happened! Not to her. She felt like throwing up afterward, but she couldn't. Her throat was dry and raspy. Thank God, he hadn't asked her to suck him off. She couldn't have done it. She would have thrown up on him.

If only she could have said no. No, I don't appreciate this. No, I don't like this. I thought you liked me. I thought you found me pretty. No. No. Why did you treat me that way? I thought you were asking me out on a date. I thought you liked me.

She'd heard that Reldie died of cancer. He'd moved out of state and had become a teacher. Maybe he'd gotten married. No one knew too much about him once he left town. No one knew the full story. It was strange to think of him being dead these twenty years. He was handsome in a rugged way, and he seemed so self-assured, so mature. That was it, he seemed so mature.

There was Wayne. She had liked him, and she thought he liked her. At a keg party by the river, they went off and started kissing. He was a poor kisser and suddenly he threw her down and started clawing at her. She couldn't believe it. He was trying to rape her! Linda fought back with all her strength and got away. She realized he was drunk. She was drinking as well, but she quickly sobered up. She had gone to the party with her girlfriend. But once Wayne attacked her, she had to leave. Her girlfriend didn't want to leave so she stayed behind. She got ride home from someone who was leaving. When she got home, she snuck in the house and went to bed with her clothes on. She locked the bedroom door. When she graduated from high school, she had bought a lock and from that day on, her room and her bed were off limits.

She was a quiet girl, but she wanted to learn about life. She wanted a boyfriend. She never dated in high school because her father wouldn't let her date. She snuck out of the house and snuck back in. When someone dropped her off on the street, she made them leave her down by the end so she could walk home. She didn't want them to see her father or mother peering through the window.

Later she decided to find a few lovers. Sadly, they weren't lovers and they taught her nothing. It was very disappointing to find that the men she picked to be her teachers were inept and selfish boys. They were all children and needed to be attended to. They all had enormous egos, and it was they who came first.

The first-person Linda fell in love with was married. That's how it happens, no? They all say they are separated from their wives and some of them might be, but most aren't. Maybe it was safe to love Gerald because he was married, unattainable, and remote. She seemed to gravitate toward men who were distant. It was easy to love him because he was so unreachable. He never told her he loved her because he didn't. He was always busy, moving from one place to another, passing through and eventually, he went away, back to his wife. She tried to love him, and he got nervous. When she pressured a man, he would leave her. Many were attracted to her, many might have wanted her to be with them, but once she got close to them, they ran away. Was she too possessive?

Linda was a passionate fuck and that was it. She wasn't girlfriend material or wife material. She was someone to be seen with, someone to go home with and then someone to be left on the street, houses away. If someone got too close to her house, she knew all hell would break loose. Her father was jealous of all her friends. Her mother didn't care about anything.

Linda. Glamorous. Exotic. A tragic beauty an acquaintance called her. She was a character out of a book or movie. Let someone make the movie. She would be the unfortunate heroine with the heartbreaking story. She would be the woman who died young, had no children, got lost in the storm, was shot in the heart, died of consumption, was lost in the ocean, fell off the mountaintop, was eaten by the lion. She was the Christian martyr who had her breasts cut off by her father who wanted to make love to her, she refused of course, and that is when he had her beheaded. He held her head on a gold platter and hung her body from the castle walls for everyone to see. She was that woman. The one who no one called girlfriend, lover, wife. Most of the time she didn't care. She just went out and got a drink or smoked weed or did some cocaine. Didn't matter she didn't have many friends, didn't matter women didn't like her and that men were afraid of her. Didn't matter if she found the perfect mate had the white picket fence that she went on vacations to Disneyland that she got invited to friend's houses for Thanksgiving and Christmas. No one invited her to birthday parties, anniversary parties. She didn't know too many children and it was good. She didn't really like children. They made her nervous. She liked being around older people. They were good to talk to. Sometimes she would drive around and end up at a nursing home. She would volunteer her time there, reading to someone or combing their hair, walking them to the lunchroom and sometimes she just listened to them talking about their lives. They played their lives over and over like a record that needed to be played again and again. She heard the music of their words and understood from them what it was like to have a life of love. Something she would never know.

And yet. . .there was always a tomorrow, wasn't there? She took another sip of her scotch and water. What did she know about life, anyway? Things changed from day to day. Who was she to know and who was she to give up. Give up? Never. Hell, she was tired.

She looked out the window at the empty street. It was going to be a cold night.

She was the one

She was the one who walked in the middle of the street

She was the who yelled at cars to drive slower

She was the one who whistled like a man

She was the one who yelled at the cars that they were driving too fast and then whistled at them and then cursed them out

She was the one who all the dogs knew.

She was the one who talked to them and told them it that it was only her, settle down, it's alright

She was the one who petted all the feral cats, knew them, and named them. Don't name them someone said, don't name them or they will keep coming back

She was the one who when Michael moved away took over his duties in the neighborhood

She was the one who monitored the street, its comings, and goings, and if ever she was to be an old lady would have told the strangers to move on, this is a family neighborhood

She was the one who longed for children

She was the one who never had children, grandchildren

She was the who used two tampons at a time

She was the one who bled so profusely, who knew that something was wrong

She was the one who had cancer of the cervix and had to have a hysterectomy when she was thirty

She was the one who had the scar tissue in her vagina and never knew it until her hysterectomy

She was the one who never dated until college

She was the one who went to Juárez to drink and dance and ate sandwiches at two in the morning at Fred's

She was the one whom the handsomest boy in high school asked to Juárez and danced and drank with her and made out in the back seat of his car and then never called her again

She was the one who thought he finally met someone nice only to have him jerk off outside his truck while she waited inside

She was the one who watched the sunset with the man who jerked off outside his truck thinking he was sensitive and nice

She was the one who persisted with this same man who wanted to play strip poker at his friends' house.

She was the one who had a strange kind of sex with this same man except he couldn't get his penis in because it was twisted

She was the one who the same man called out to his friend and said she was easy

She was the one who certain man called an easy lay

She was the one who wasn't an easy lay

She was the one who should have known better

She was the one who kept trying to find someone who would treat her well

She was the one who made out with the visiting cousin from up north because she was drunk

She was the one who wore the wiglet that the visiting cousin tried to put his fingers through

She was the one who felt like a fool for wearing a wiglet and for making out with the visiting cousin

She was the one who fell asleep with her false eyelashes on and had trouble opening her eyes in the morning

She was the one who loved to kiss

She was the one who kissed so much her jaw was sore

She was the one who could have only kissed

She was the one who certain man were ashamed of kissing

She was the one who men liked but never loved

She was the one who mostly had male friends

She was the one who had few female friends

She was the one who women never called

She was the one who would have loved to have more friends, especially women

She was the one who was always hurt when no one called her, invited her out and only thought of including her if she was there, in front of them

She was the one who loved to dance

She was the one who was a great dancer

She was the one who loved to drink

She was the one who loved to get drunk

She was the one who could hold their liquor

She was the one who drank like a man

She was the one who should have been a man

She was the one who was born a woman

She was the one who imagined that if she had been born a man, she would have been a good man, not like all the men she'd met or known

She was the one who often regretted she was a woman

She was the one who was the woman all the men wanted but not in daylight

She was the woman who would have made an excellent wife and mother if anyone had ever seen her as a wife and mother

She was the one who tried to control her life

She was the one who decided early on that she would learn how to make love so she could be a good lover

She was the one who experimented with various lovers and found them all lacking

She was the one who shouldn't have been looking for a man who would love her

She was the one who never gave up looking for a man who would love her

She was the one who could never find a man to love her

She was the one who tried too hard

She was the one who everyone thought was lively, lovely, and a bit too sad

She was the one who wondered why no one respected her enough, cared for her enough, appreciated her enough

She was the one who was a true and loyal friend

Yes, she was the one, she was that and more

She was the one who worked hard, played hard, lived hard, and probably would die hard

She was the one who always won the bets

She was the one who beat the odds

She was the one who had luck with cards

She was the one had the luck with horses

She was the one who dogs came up to, cats sidled near

She was the one who made the babies stop crying

She was the one who made the old women start gossiping

She was the one who old men loved to talk to

She was the one sat by herself at the parties

She was the one who left with the handsomest man

She was the one who arrived home late, alone

She was the one who walked in the middle of the street

She was the one who whistled loudly when someone drove too fast, too recklessly

She was the one who would give you the finger if you deserved it, no matter who you were or what age

She was the one who believed in justice, dignity, and equality for all

She was the one who fought for strangers and sometimes got in fights

She was the one who learned the hard way

She was the one who was your best friend if you allowed her to be

She was the woman who scared women

She was the woman who scared men

She was the woman who scared herself

She was the one who hated waiting

She was the one who had to wait

She was the one who graduated with honors

She was the one who was an excellent student

She was the one who was one who never won awards and should have

She was the one who deserved more, got less

She was the one who anyone would have said, she will go far, she will become something, be someone

She was the one who was a good daughter
She was the one who was a good sister
She was the one who was a lovely child
She was the one who was a beautiful woman
She was the one who was full of hope
She was the one who was full of fear
She was the one who was talented and brave and timid all at
the same time
She was the one who depended on others and shouldn't have
She was the one who depended on too many men
She was the one who depended on that woman, her mother,
and she shouldn't have
She was the one who should have left home, and she didn't
She was the one who left and left and kept coming back
She was the one who anyone might have said: Linda. Linda.
She's very polite. Very sweet
She was the one who wasn't. Polite. Sweet
She was the one who was more than anyone ever imagined
She was the one to be admired. Of all the people on the street,
that street that once was home. Home to so many. She was the One
Where are they now? Where have they gone?
She was the One
She whistled like a man
She walked in the middle of the street
The street belonged to her
Those other people?
They only lived in the houses

The moon was rimmed in shadows. There was a strange and beautiful light that shone on the street. It was quiet and dark. Few cars came by at this time of day. The heaviest traffic was in the morning and after work. This is when people were rushing to get to work, rushing to get home, rushing. Linda felt happy. No reason. Maybe because Christmas was coming, and Thanksgiving was over. She didn't like turkey. She never had liked the taste. The whole concept of Thanksgiving was repulsive to her. Maybe that wasn't the word. Distasteful. People gathering family as if they were family and loved each other. This year she'd been invited to eat lunch at the Stillman's house. Clemson was there with his wife and his girlfriend. Michael was there with his new friend, a very large woman with a huge ass. Linda couldn't help but notice her butt. Anyone would. Why Michael had invited her, she couldn't guess. She didn't know he was going to have a date. Ha! He never had dates just like she never had dates. The big-assed woman was his latest big-assed one. She seemed nice enough, but everyone avoided her. As far as she could tell, the only one who really conversed with her was Michael. Conversed, quaint word. What did they talk about? She seemed so out of his league, so disjointed from the present company. Thank God his mother was deceased. His father Bobby was an old man now and one of God's chosen, a deacon in the church, so he loved everyone. The people that were at the lunch were mostly Mona's friends. Mona was Clem's wife, and her friends were an odd assortment of dried-out Anglo women who were once teachers or librarians (she was a school nurse) or a few neighbors like Linda, who Mona just happened to run into. How about coming over, she said. Michael will be there. You went to school with him, didn't you?

No, Mona, Linda thought. We were alcoholics together and then he got straight, and I kept going to AA and then I got straight, and he was still straight and then we saw each other a few times as friends and then one cold night like this one we went back to his place for tea, and I ended up staying the night. It was a grave mistake. I should have never touched him. Once I untucked his shirt, I knew I was sunk. It's not that I loved him, no I didn't love him. And he didn't love me, but he could have if I'd given him a chance. I never gave him a chance. I didn't want to give him a chance. If I did, I might want to love him. But I couldn't and he couldn't.

The last time I saw him he was with a woman who was much older than he was. She was very nice, lovely in her own way. A lady. He should have stayed with her. She was good to him, and they seemed happy for a while. He didn't date many ladies like that one. Most of the women he showed up with were odd. Displaced. Too young too old too loud too soft too serious too silly. And he was too much for them. He used them and then he discarded them. The 4 F's. Find them. Feel them. Fuck them. Forget them. He weren't no good with women. Never was. He could never find his match. Same reason I never married.

And there we were around that large table with a giant turkey in the middle. A ham on this side and all the usual food displayed and ready to be eaten. Mashed potatoes and gravy, green beans with Campbell's soup topping, candied yams with marshmallows. The pies on another table did look good. I wish I had brought something. No one told me. Mona should have mentioned something. Maybe it didn't matter, she was so used to doing everything by herself. Old Clemson was serving drinks and when I got up to get a soda and some ice, he started in. Here he was with his wife in the other room and his girlfriend helping in the kitchen and the wife not knowing or caring and him coming on to the young girls, his nieces and cousins and anyone else he wanted to get close to. And there was Michael with that woman with the huge butt who wasn't his type at all.

I ate fast and went home and went to bed. It was that kind of day. The cold gets stronger each day. Nothing to do about it.

I had to get up because I started itching. Usually this happens when I eat bad fish. I mean what kind of fish can you find in the desert? Restaurants must fly it in frozen and when it's thawed that's when all hell breaks loose. I stopped eating fish for this reason. I can't trust any of it will be fresh.

It might have been the turkey. Who knows. It was an unpleasant afternoon, and I should have never gone over there. I thought I might visit with Michael. He was the only one there I could have talked to, the only one who could hold a conversation about interesting things. The only cultured person. Except he forgot how to be cultured. He forgot how to be who he was. I didn't recognize him. He was another person. He started to look more like his brother. And I forgot what he was like when I knew him in the past. I remembered him from those days when we used to talk for hours about things that mattered to us.

I'm not sure what it was. These days I can't eat anything without bloating up. I feel as if someone has punched me in the stomach and then driven their clenched fist upward into my solar plexus. My chest is tight, and my rib cage feels compressed. And then sometimes my right lower side hurts and I wonder if it's my kidneys or liver. I can't remember where my organs are anymore and need to look them up. And then it's that spot on the back side of my lung, on the lower right that started hurting long ago when I met Gerald. Here's to old lovers. Here's the stories that stayed with your body. Here's to the pains that seemed to leave and then came back. The stories that you never forgot and tried to. Thinking of that man that should have loved me. What happened to him? Maybe he died. I wonder about that. Not sure I can read the story about his life anywhere. Where can you find the stories of those people who left us? You look in the obituary columns, but you can't find them there. You ask people who knew you then and who knew them then. Haven't heard about him they say. Don't know what happened to him. We lost touch. And you think you should know in your skin if they are dead or not. Because any woman knows that the DNA of every man, she's made love to stays in her skin, in her vagina and in her brain. So, is he dead? And if so, when did he die? And if not, where he is?

Looking for you, Carl. Wondering what happened Earl. Know you passed away Sam. Wife left you. You left your family. Your sister was killed. Mother died of grief. Father was in an accident, never recovered. Died in her sleep. Died at home. Died surrounded by his children. Surrounded by her loved ones. Died alone. Died in the summer. Died in the winter. Died in a time like this.

The moon was surrounded by a shadow. It was a hazy foggy moon and if you stood on the sidewalk the street looked wet, but it wasn't. The steam rose and it was quiet, but you heard the sounds underneath the sounds. The older you get, the more you hear the underside of life. You hear things you shouldn't hear. You see things you shouldn't see. There is a spirit cat that comes out once and a while and crosses the street. She is very old and once lived nearby. You wonder when. Perhaps it was in the late 1800s. The cat likes the neighborhood and she's friendly. She isn't afraid of you but she's a bit shy. She was a mama cat, and her kittens are now all gone. Only she stayed behind. And sometimes when you least expect, she will come out and say hello.

And then there's the voice of the man who speaks to you early in the morning. Where did he come from and what does he have to say? And why is he here? He's not welcome.

You start to hear voices and you begin to see things. But what's new? This was how it was then, and this is still how it is now.

You feel itchy and wonder what it could be? The food? The noises in the background that are becoming louder. The spirits who rub up against you and the cat who is looking for her kittens.

Where are those people you once knew? Once loved?

The nights are a confusion of dreams. You are looking for something still. You are lost and locked out. You can't find your way. You need to climb down. You need to get up. You are locked in or locked out.

The old stories. You find yourself on the street again trying to find your way home. Always home.

Okay, keep going. It isn't far. Someone will come along with a key. Someone will come around the bend to help you. You count on that. You count on that. The merciful stranger.

Almost there. You walk down the street again. The moon rimmed in wonder. That bright star someone calling out to you. Who is it? Mother? Father?

Oh, it's you.

She wanted to dance. Really dance. There were so few people that knew how to dance. They hadn't been primed since they were children. They didn't dance at home. They didn't dance at school. Their sisters or brothers didn't dance with them. Nuns taught them how to dance. They learned to do folk dances from around the world once a week. They didn't play at their house. They didn't pretend they were diving as they jumped on their bed. They didn't play or prance around when company came over. They didn't have company. Their parents didn't entertain. What few social skills they had they'd learned from a few people—a teacher, a neighbor, a stranger.

And yet, they were dancers. They could and wanted to dance. They had rhythm. They knew what it was to let go. A lo todo dar. And they did this in dancing. In singing. In writing. In cooking. In doing the things they loved most in the world.

Voices could be heard. Victoria! Don't let me die, Mundo pleaded. Adoración moaned and Adelaida came to attend to her. Down the street a woman was dying. Ay, vieja cabrona, ayúdame she shouted. The old lady had moved into the neighborhood and was always cruel to her maids, yelling at them in an ugly Spanish in her nasty, raspy, uncouth voice. She cried hard and then screamed, Chole, Chole! Llama a mi hija. And poor Chole went through the motions. The old lady's daughter was always out of town, never wanted to be bothered. And the old lady gasped and gurgled in mortal fear and Chole didn't know what to do. The death rattle overtook the old lady, and she screamed in agony. Chole didn't know anyone on the street to call except for Senaida. But Senaida didn't want to help, she just said, let her die, she's an old woman, and she was mean to everyone, just let her die. Just let her die! Chole whimpered, in agony. Have you seen someone die in front of you who is terrified? Isn't there something we can do, someone we can call?

Was she Catholic? Senaida asked. No, I don't think so, Chole said, trying to remember. No, I don't think so. Well then, Senaida said, I don't know of any preachers that come out in the middle of the night to pray over a Protestant. There's one good thing about being Catholic—the priests will always come out, day or night, anytime of the day. Oh, then let's call a priest, Chole begged. No, I don't think so. She wasn't Catholic and her daughter Socorro wouldn't like it. Who cares, who cares, Chole thought, but she knew it was true. Chole went back into the old lady's room and watched her writhing on the bed in terrible anguish. How long the night is—how long the night is on this street of pain! Chole didn't have the phone numbers of anyone to call. And Socorro, ay, she never wants to be bothered. What to do this inexorable night of passage, the coldest night of this month so far, and Chole with the old lady dying without family?

Linda coughed into a Kleenex and there was blood. Not much, but still it was there. It's not the first time.

The wind was full of voices.

Senaida yelled to Joe that she hated him and regretted everything. You trapped me he yelled back. Yes, she yelled again. I was pregnant. No, you weren't, that's what you always say. You weren't pregnant and you know it. You trapped me, woman. That's all there is to it.

I was.

No, you weren't.

I was, goddamn it.

Erme cried in desperation and then fell on the floor writhing and crying. When she was overwrought, she rolled around on the floor, scaring Victoria. Was her mother having a seizure, she wondered. Is she dying? Erme was beside herself and couldn't believe Mundo had left her and Victoria. Why? What had she done?

What had she done to deserve this life? Lety wondered. Bobby asked the same question. He loved Lety but she was too hard. Lety loved Bobby but he was too soft. They were so happy early on, what happened? Too many children, too many heartaches, not enough money to live well or the right way. Always worrying about money and bills and more bills and food and school and then there was Adoración. No one to help her really. Sometimes her sister, sometimes her sister-in-law, sometimes no one. Sometimes the children and then sometimes a maid. Maids cost money no matter how much you pay them. Best to find an old one who doesn't go out and buy clothes and who wants to go home every weekend to her family and has a boyfriend or starts flirting with your son or your brother. The young ones are whores or could be. Best to hire an old woman but she needs to be strong and young enough to lift and bend. And she needs to be quiet and not talk back like the young ones who you must train. All the maids have worn me out. You can't get good help anymore. I should know. I've never really had good help. There was Adelaida but then Maggie took her away. She started paying her more money and Adelaida never wanted to come back after that. You can't spoil maids. If you pay them too much, they get spoiled and want more. You need to start low and stay low. And if you don't go up a little bit now and then, they'll find a new patrona. Good ahead, I say, let them. They're spoiled. They should be grateful they have a job, food, a roof over their heads. What do they have in México but a cardboard shack for ten people to a room? All my maids had it good, only they didn't know it. I don't understand it, really. They should be grateful for any job. What do they have in México? Nothing. Poverty and more poverty. I've been there, I've seen how they live.

Sometimes the voices were loud, sometimes they whispered and sometimes they cried the way people cry in other places and in other languages. The word llanto is weeping in Spanish but a llanto is more sorrowful than a cry. It is more powerful than a few tears and when you hear someone lament the way they did in the past of a life lived, you can't help but feel a chill.

The nights were cold and getting colder. No one on the street made fires anymore. Too busy. Too hard to get firewood. Too distracted. Too messy. No one had time to rest. Nearly every house had a fireplace, but no one used them anymore. And yet, they all loved the fires that allowed them to rest a bit, to sit in the darkness of their living rooms or dens and see the shadows on the walls. And when the fire was burned down, they went to bed and slept through the night, at peace because sitting by a fire will do that to you. They will bring you a peace that is good and needed.

When I die, I'll rest, Lety thought. Someday when I'm long gone, I'll sleep all day in that other world, and I'll be alone in my own house on the other side. I won't have so many children or any children and maybe I'll be a man. It might be easier she thought. None of the business of a woman's body. I've surely had enough of bleeding and bearing. I could go on, but I won't. Let's just say I had enough.

The train whistle began from the south and moved north. It was night and this is when most trains came through. The street led to the train tracks and yes, it was hard living on that street if you hated trains coming through at all times during the night. Somehow, after a while, you got used to the long whistle and the sound of metal hitting the track. The echo of the train was sometimes sad and sometime soothing. If you were young and in love with someone who was far away, the noise of any train brought sorrow. If you were older, the sound of the train reminded you of that time of loving too much. How foolish we were to have loved so hard and so recklessly and so stupidly! So much time wasted! Too many nights of madness and what did it bring us anyway, after all? It brought us the stories, but who cares about them anyway? Most of the stories of the world are untold and unappreciated anyway. So what use was it, mother? Why did we bother, father? Your sister's story—unconfirmed, unreported. Your brother's story for naught. The tragic deaths a history. The suicides washed over, dismissed. The stories were just that, stories. Who listened to them anyway? And if you spoke the truth, you were drowned out by the train and then the wind.

Still, out there, in the street, the stories spun round, traveled fast, moved through the trees up to the sky and headed farther out where there was darkness and then light. After all, they were not stories but spirits that once lived and loved and then moved on. And where they went, well, how am I to know? My story is yet to be told, Linda thought. And who will be there to tell my story? Will anyone remember me other than those few?

Those men and women heard my story in that hot and humid room as we declared our sins to each other. In the confessional of my alcoholism and my shame I remembered that I was no better and no worse than anyone in that room where we admitted to each other that we had lied, deceived, belittled, and inflicted pain not only on ourselves but on those closest to us. Father forgive me for I have sinned. Mother forgive me for I have lied. Countless times I have lied to you and to myself. Brother forgive me for deceiving and using you, sister forgive me for violating your body and spirit. And you, forgive me for not caring for you enough and for negating the life of my own self. I ask myself for forgiveness.

Now stop there. Just stop.

This story is just that. Story.

Today is not the day. There are days for living and days for dying. Today was not a day for dying.

Linda was fostering a small, yellow-colored kitten that was about five weeks old. It was hard to tell as the kitten was so diminished. It had an eye infection and was very dehydrated. The worst thing was that its right back hind left was working. It just hung there like an appendage of flesh. The little cat dragged itself across the room. She had offered to help a student at the university who found the cat and wondered if Linda could help. No, but yes. Who wouldn't help a small life? But after going to see the vet, the prognosis got worse. The cat needed surgery. It would be costly to repair the pelvis if it could be repaired. She waited to hear from the surgeon who worked out of town.

She named the kitten Sammy.

When you devote time to animals you come to understand the real suffering of the world. You come to understand what it is to be a child and helpless. You come to understand how much every one of us needs to support life, at all costs. To give life a try. Darle el try she heard someone once say. Dale el Try.

How pitiful she had become, and how negative and self-absorbed! And the same went for all the people she had come to call friends. Why wasn't she out there in the world doing good, working for others, helping children, animals, the elderly? She could barely help herself, but she could help others. Why not?

Dale el try.

How to begin?

Watching little Sammy as he lay there resting, her heart went out to all creatures, great and small. How precious their lives are. How much they had to teach us if only we could listen to their stories.

The street had its stories. The animals who were chained and tied up for too long called out to her. Her neighbor's dogs never ran on grass or even on cement. They were never taken out of the backyard and given their freedom. They barked in recognition of who she was, and she called back to them. It's just me. Rest. Relax.

Little Sammy stirred. He was a small broken cat, but he had a will to live, a desire to thrive. What had happened to him? Was he hit by a car, did he fall from a height, was he attacked by a dog? With animals there was no way of knowing their suffering. They speak but silently, without words.

The little cats gathered at night for her, and it gave her joy. Someone was waiting for her out there in the darkness. She called them out by name, and they answered back. They knew her and she knew them.

Walking back home from feeding her cats she reflected on the nature of suffering. We are of the nature to age. We are of the nature to get sick. We are of the nature to die. Buddhism had taught her much and she loved the work of the Vietnamese Buddhist monk, Thich Nhat Hanh.

She would hold little Sammy in her arms and sing to it a special song she had made up for those special little animals in her life. Little baby Sammy. Little baby boy. The cats liked hearing her sing just to them. Each cat had a different version and yet, the rhythm was the same. It was the underlying rhythm of her love. And that rhythm came and went and swelled with passion and then subsided with her pain. How could she keep her song alive when all around her was so much suffering?

What could she do for the people on her little street? Many of them were gone now and strangers lived in their houses. No one remembered the summer nights when they were children and their fathers strung up piñatas and invited all the neighborhood children to come and eat banana and peanut butter sandwiches. No one re-membered old lady Romero who had cancer and who smelled like Vicks and old dusty rags. The kids made fun of her, the way she walked. There were religious men and saintly women on the street, they prayed the rosary in the summertime in their backyards, as the children fidgeted and couldn't wait to get away. The adults were full of intention and tried to be good. Some were successful and others not. Some never wanted to be good. Most everyone just wanted to get away. Get a life. Leave the street. Leave town. Find jobs. Get a career. Make money. Have a family. Make money. Make money.

Linda never knew what money was about. With her, it came and went. She was still the little girl whose father gave her a quarter and cried when she had to spend it. She wanted to spend her father's quarters, not hers. She was never a businesswoman, never took accounting or could handle her checkbook. And yet, she tried. She had traveled all over the world, had a successful life, maybe, for a while, but where was everything now?

She sat in the room with Sammy. He was stirring. Was he hungry? Poor little broken thing. Would he survive? Yes, he would. He had to. She was counting on it. Praying for it. He might be lame on one side. He might be without a leg. He would never be an outside cat. He would never know what it was to run and jump, but then again, maybe he would. To give up on life wasn't good. Today was not the day to give up give in. Here she was, gone down that street so far and she'd never gone anywhere. She still lived at home. But her home had changed. Now it was her home. She didn't have a lock on her bedroom door. All the doors were kept open the way her mother wished. Now she realized why her mother wanted the doors open all the time. She was afraid when people closed their doors. How she wished she could go back and hold her mother and maybe they'd cry together. A good long cry between women who understood.

You knew?

Yes.

Did you?

Yes.

I forgive you.

The street knew the stories and it forgave the people. It didn't judge them. The street knew who had been hurt and who had hurt them. It knew their lives. It saw everything.

Things were simple today. Yesterday was another day and it was hard. Linda's stomach had hurt her for so long and then she had pains all over and sometimes they were concentrated in different places. She took a bath and wept and then she sang very loudly. No one heard her. It was a good thing. She remembered Adelaida wailing at the funeral of Adoración. She had been there and how could she forget the cry of that woman and how it filled the church. People still talked about the day the old Mexican woman carried on in church and how awful it was.

What had happened to Adelaida? She eventually went back to her people. She was only here for a short while. She was traveling through. Una pasajera. She went back to her life and her street and her people. But she left something of herself with the people she had lived with. There was a trace, a spark of energy, a light that emanated from her life and the street still held the memory.

The street was small. It went nowhere really but back around the corner. It led to the main streets of the city. It was a nothing street. Not important. It wasn't a fancy or well-kept street. Its houses were once middle-class, but now they were poor, run down, full of strange and unusual characters, the two men who were always bringing things out their garage apartment. Possibly stolen goods. In Sen's old house lived a couple who hung a tulle party dress from the front porch, winter, or summer the pink and white dress was there. Did they know the history of the house? Had they heard of the wedding dress that hung in the living room until one day it just disappeared? Who were those people and where was Sen? Where was Joe?

Was he in another world reading the newspaper there?

In a dream Linda visited what might have been heaven, but it wasn't. It was a city full of temples and the temples had turrets of gold and domes that sparkled and shone in the sun. Linda flew over the city of gold and marveled at its incredible beauty. Where was this place? Had she once lived there or would she in future?

She had no answers.

What she remembered now and what she would always remember would be her little street. Her little town. The people she had known, their stories.

Sammy was sleeping peacefully. Who knew what his little life would be? What mattered was now.

Today was not the day. Or you might say that today was the day.

It was getting late. But it was still early for the street. The street still had stories to tell. Its spirits still had houses to visit, people to see and comfort, and places to rest before and after that journey from that other world.

A child ran through the street with his dog calling out excitedly, "Pasajero, Pasajero!" both of them happy, free. From the street you could see a large piñata that swayed and bobbled and then fell with the last hit from the wooden stick as children raced to gather the bounteous candy that tumbled to the ground. A beautiful young woman lit a candle in her bedroom on an altar for the ancestors who stood nearby. Suddenly she was back in her village in México standing next to her mother and her grandmother. It was Día de Muertos and there was homage to be paid. Love to be celebrated. Prayers to be chanted. Prayers that brought solace, relief. Dulce corazón de María, sálvame.

Inside a quiet house a woman read a book, beside her a cup of strong hot coffee. She was content. No one was there to bother or interrupt her, to demand things of her, her time was all her time. A young man lay in bed, tossing and tumbling with the one he loved. He heard noises outside and thought he should get up to see what was happening. But no. What was happening outside didn't matter, not at that moment. Inside another house, a young woman danced with a small child, a little girl who shrieked with laughter, both of them enthralled, caught in that moment of joy. A small cat watched it all from the window ledge, peaceful, purring. She could see all that was happening out there in that other world, and it was fine with her. She was comfortable where she was. Near, but distant. Present but not preoccupied.

Music of all types could be heard all at once, a cacophony of sound, until that one song was left, filling the air with memory.

Everyone heard their favorite song. Maybe it was Jerry Vale's, You Don't Know Me or Frank Sinatra's My Way. The Little Drummer Boy echoed down the Street bringing much joy to many.

An old woman finished her rosary for those she loved on this earth and in the spirit realm, and then commenced to braid her long thin hair into a trenza as she sang Bendito, Bendito. Bendito Sea Dios. Soon she would go to bed singing.

Perhaps it was the haunting Camino de Guanajuato by José Alfredo Jiménez or that exultant Mexican ranchera, Volver, Volver. The songs faded in and out and then blended one into another until an exultant and hearty grito filled the street with longing and lust for life as the man in the bedroom faced his lover. ¡Ayyyy!

It was summer for some, winter for others, it was all time and no time. There was no hurry. Nothing to be done with nothing left undone. You could move through walls if you wished or fly up to the sky. The sunset went on forever and it was so glorious it filled the sky with pink and blue and over there, there was a break of cloud that led further and higher upward toward the mystery of purple gold.

A stranger passed by with all his possessions in a shopping cart wrapped in a white sheet. He was still alive and didn't see the others out there in the street dancing. Soon he would.

The spirits spiraled and twirled and called out greetings to each other. Hola! Buenos Días le de Dios! How are you doing? ¿Qué hay de nuevo? No, me digas. Ay mi'jita, I love you. Come on now, give me your hands, let's dance! I love you, baby. Precious. Precious.

The spirits swayed and leapt and laughed and carried on. The men that had been men the women that had been women the dogs the cats all of them. Travelers. Pasajeros. They danced inside their homes or ventured out into the street and moved on to visit other places, other spirits. They could do as they wished. Whatever they wished. Or they could stay where they were. They had that choice. Some stayed behind to see what was happening, what would unfold, to help others, to assist as they could, to leave that feather or that rock or that piece of paper behind as testimony or a note of love. On it written nearly invisible words only to be read by those who could read, the songs heard by those that could hear the melancholy faraway song, those that witnessed and celebrated the imperceptible signs, those who saw understood believed.

The spirits danced. The way they do when they are free. The way they do when they are happy. Bodiless. Unbounded by pain. Complete. Fulfilled. Unfettered. Free.

It was a beautiful thing to see—*if* you could see it.

ABOUT THE AUTHOR

DENISE CHÁVEZ is a Fronteriza writer, bookseller, and activist for Sentient Life. She is the owner, with her husband, Franco/Ukranian/American photographer, Daniel Zolinsky, of Casa Camino Real Bookstore in Las Cruces, New Mexico. It is located in the historic Mesquite District and on the Camino Real.

Chávez is the author of *The King and Queen of Comezón*; *Loving Pedro Infante*; *A Taco Testimony: Meditations on Family, Food and Culture*; *Face of An Angel*; and *The Last of the Menu Girls*.

She has a BA in Theatre and English from New Mexico State University (1971), an MFA in Theatre from Trinity University (1974), an MFA in Creative Writing from the University of New Mexico (1984), and an Honorary Doctorate from the University of New Mexico (2004).

Chávez has received various awards, including the the New Mexico Governor's Award, The American Book Award, the Premio Aztlán Literary Prize, and the Hispanic Heritage Award in Literature, among others.

Chávez is the Director and Co/Founder of Libros Para El Viaje/Books for the Journey, an ongoing book gathering and distribution initiative that delivers books to Refugee, Migrant, and Asylum-seekers children and families on the U.S./México border, schools, libraries, unhoused apartments, Senior Centers, El Caldito Soup kitchen, and other places in need of books.

Chávez's long-term project, Museo de La Gente/Museum of the People, is the formation of a community archival resource center, library, bookstore, and living archive of the Borderland region. It will be based in her hometown of Las Cruces, New Mexico.

CONOCIMIENTOS
PRESS

TESTIMONIOS & NON-FICTION

Rooted in Clay: Verónica Castillo y su arte (2023)
Josie Méndez-Negrete

Home, Where Memories Wait to be Remembered (2022)
Teresa Villarreal Rodriguez

*Crossing Borders, Building Bridges:
A Journalist's Heart in Latin America* (2020)
Maria E. Martin

The Art of Mariachi: A Curriculum Guide (2017)
Dr. Rachel Yvonne Cruz

Women, Mujeres, Ixoq: Revolutionary Visions (2017)
Claudia D. Hernández

FICTION

Antonio: A Mexican Boy & His Stories (2023)
Jesse Natal Sánchez

A Street of Too Many Stories (2024)
Denise Chávez

CHILDREN'S BOOKS

Dexter the Ducken (2021)
Alette Lundeberg with Illustrations by ash good

Grandpa Lee's Stories: New Mexico to California (2020)
Helen Najera Reyes with Illustrations by Hector Garza.

Love and Monsters in Sofia's Life / Amor y Monstruos en la Vida de Sofía (2020)
Belinda Hernández Arriaga with Illustrations by Verónica Castillo Salas
Spanish Translation by Josie Méndez-Negrete

CONOCIMIENTOSPRESSLLC.COM

www.ingramcontent.com/pod-product-compliance
Lightning Source LLC
Chambersburg PA
CBHW061542310726
48972CB00008B/2568